A Case for Her Heart

Kristen Taylor

Thank You So Much

To my mom who pushed me to write this book, but also knew that I would genuinely enjoy writing what I wanted to read.

To my friends who read the chapters that I had no idea how to write, and gave me advice. (Except I doubt my guy friends would see this)

A huge, huge, huge, thank you to my editing partner Lydia Emrath. You're absolutely amazing for putting up with me and helping me edit. Oh and also helping me figure out quite a bit of the plot. You're awesome!

And the biggest person I want to say thank you to is God. Thank you for giving me the knowledge, the time, the energy, and the gift to be able to even write this book.

Dedicated to...

To my girls who adore reading, (and maybe romanticizing some cute boys), but also want to keep everything clean. I love you guys so much, and I think this book is definitely something to check out.

Chapter 1

"*D*ispatch to two-seventeen and one-thirty-four."

All I can do is groan at the sound of the radio. Picking it up, I speak into it to confirm my presence, "Two-seventeen to dispatch."

Inside my car, silence fills the air while I wait for a response from the second officer I am on duty with tonight. I am absolutely not looking forward to this late-night call, especially if it's from someone who's being overdramatic.

The radio crackles to life, "One-thirty-four to dispatch"

"We have a PC four-five-nine at twenty-six forty-two Allen Street," the dispatcher reports back to me. *A burglary? Really?*

Snapping out of my silent annoyance, I answer, "10-4. En route from Rosewood and Fifth. My ETA is around fifteen minutes." With that, I start the car and begin to drive toward the neighborhood I am instructed to investigate.

When the radio crackles to life again, I hear the other officer confirm, "10-4. Enroute from Blackthorn and Main. My ETA is around twenty to twenty-five minutes."

While driving there, my mind goes straight into autopilot, every single part of my body aching, ready to head home. *Nope, you have to take this call. It's quite literally part of your job.*

As I pull onto the street, the dispatcher asks me again what my ETA is. I respond by telling her that I have just pulled up to the house. The dispatcher gives me the rest of the information she gathered during the call, "There should be a woman at twenty-six forty waiting for you. She reports that no weapons are involved. We have informed her that you will be the one speaking to her"

"Copy."

When I catch sight of a woman anxiously pacing her driveway, I park the car, quickly checking for the correct address. Confirming my location to the dispatcher, I get out of my car, holding up my badge, and address the woman who looks to be in her mid-forties, "Hello ma'am, I'm Officer Adria Sousa. What seems to be the issue here?"

"Good evening, my apologies for the late-night call. I happened to stay up waiting for my son to come home when I caught sight of a figure breaking into twenty-six forty-two," she responds slightly panicked.

Immediately, I assume that the person "breaking" into the house was just the homeowner who left their keys at home. But when I ask the woman about it, she seems offended that I would even doubt her.

"There's just no way that what I saw was my neighbor who forgot her keys. The family who lives there are on vacation for their kids' winter break. I've been house-sitting and dog-sitting for them this past week. I was at the house around three hours ago."

Nodding as I write down the information she's giving me, I then ask for the key to the house, assuring the woman that I am going to check out the situation.

Shoot there's a dog inside the house too. I hope it's a smaller one. Sighing, I open the door, half-expecting a giant dog to try and jump on me or something. But instead, I was

2

met with darkness and silence. *Weird. The dog didn't even bark.*

"Silver Valley Police!" I bellow, Glock 48 out, hoping that there is no one inside the house, but ready in case there is.

When nothing happens, including a dog barking, I pick up the radio and report, "Received house key from the neighbor, one-thirty-four, the door will be unlocked."

"Copy"

With that, I start walking through the first level of the house searching for evidence of a break-in. Everything in this house was neatly put away, a thin layer of dust covering the windowsills, the piano in the living room, and the TV. Before walking away from the living room, I check the windows, which are unsurprisingly locked.

Going through the kitchen, and the bathroom continues to confirm that this house has been basically unlived in, besides their neighbor coming in to feed the dog. Speaking of which, I still haven't seen the dog yet. But when I go to check the back door, it is unlocked. It doesn't look like the door is forced open though. Quickly, I walk outside just to make sure that no one is there. Honestly, I think the neighbor probably just left the door unlocked when she went outside.

Moving towards the garage, I open the creaky door looking for a sign of forced entry but find nothing again. Confused, I leave the garage and decide to head upstairs to check the bedrooms too.

There are three rooms. Two are immediately visible, and another is down the hallway. Walking into the first two rooms only confirms that there really has been no one living in the house for a week. In fact, it doesn't look like anyone has even touched these two rooms in a minute.

Once I finish inspecting the first two bedrooms, I start walking down the hall to the final one, but something catches my eye. There is a dim light seeping from the cracked open door. Cautiously, I continue walking towards the room. Taking a deep breath, I place a hand on my gun before yelling out, "Silver Valley Police! Weapons down, and come out where I can see you! Hands up where I can see them!"

When nothing happens, I carefully open the door, expecting to be met with nothing. But what I see only makes my heart drop. There is a cocker spaniel with a knife stuck through its chest. Blood is seeping out of the poor dog from its stab wounds. *Crap. Someone was in here.*

Running, I start to check in the closets, and under the bed. "Anyone in this room, out with your hands above your head where I can see them!"

As I check the bed, I hear the front door open, but before I can say anything, I hear a rustle in the closet. I quickly head over to the closet, hand on my gun, and open the closet door, to see a young man hiding in the closet.

Quickly reacting, I guide him out, switching my hold from a gun to a taser when I see he's not holding anything, "Hands up where I can see them!"

The door decides to burst open as I'm leading the guy out of the closet. I turn around, still holding the taser towards the man to see my partner for the night. Facing the culprit again, I hear Officer Perez speaking into the radio reporting what's happening. When he's done doing that, I continue to hold the taser up while he handcuffs the man. Sighing, we both lead him to the wall before patting him down. I find several necklaces and a wad of cash.

After checking to make sure that the young man is leaving with Officer Perez, I quickly run to the patrol car while reporting to dispatch, "I'm going to need a clean-up crew to clean up the blood spilled on the carpet. We have detained the burglar, and Officer Perez will bring back the caught burglar to the station. I will stay here until the clean-up crew arrives, and gather the evidence for the report."

The radio crackles as the dispatcher speaks, "Copy. I'll send the clean-up crew over right now. We will have a cell waiting for him when Officer Perez returns to the station. How long ago did he leave?"

"He left around five minutes ago."

"Copy. Clean-up crew's ETA is in an hour."

After confirming that I will stay, I quickly grab a pair of gloves and some bags for evidence before running right back inside the house. While working on gathering the fingerprints and the knife, I hear the doorbell ring. As I walk downstairs, the clock catches my eye, and I notice it's already five a.m. *Oh, dear Lord. I just want to go home.*

Before even looking at the crew, I start my introduction spiel, "Hi. I'm Officer Sousa. The room that we need to have cleaned up is the one farthest down the hall. There's a light on in that room while the other two rooms upstairs don't have any lights on. In the room, there is the corpse of a dog, along with a decent amount of blood splatters. Please clean up the blood on the carpet, place the knife that was used to strike the dog in an evidence bag, and dispose of the dog's body."

The lead of the clean-up crew responds, being polite, "Good morning Officer Sousa. My name is Jennett. I will tell the rest of the crew your instructions before they head up to clean the blood. No one was hurt other than the dog I presume."

All I do is nod before leading her upstairs. Honestly, it might've been rude, but I was so tired, I couldn't bring myself to care.

As Jennett leads her team into the room, she exclaims when she sees the dog, "Oh? What's this? That poor dog. How could someone be so cruel to this adorable little thing? Well, we're here to clean everything up. Do you have all the things you need to make a report and possibly an investigation on this before we start cleaning up this room?"

5

"I have everything I need from this room, thank you. I will be either downstairs by the backdoor, or the garage looking for any other materials we can use for the report. Please let me know when you are finished."

"You got it, Officer." Jannett all but cheers as she starts to clean up the mess with the rest of her crew. *Her enthusiasm is borderline sickening.*

Before walking downstairs, I quickly scan the other two upstairs bedrooms for any sign of breaking and entering. *What I'd give to lay down in that bed right now. Whelp. Time to get back to work so I can actually sleep soon.*

The backdoor, I remember, is unlocked, so I head outside to the door and start collecting the fingerprints on the door handle. Once I'm done, I just walk through the rest of the house looking for anywhere the burglar could have searched. I look for over twenty minutes, but in the end, it's evidently clear that he only broke into the master bedroom.

That annoyingly chipper voice breaks through my thoughts, "Alright! We're done cleaning up the room. It's as good as new. The dog's body will be brought back with us, and then there is the knife in the evidence bag as you requested." I try my best not to make a face as she hands me the evidence bag. From the way her smile slightly falters I'd say I still look annoyed, if not slightly pissed off.

Thanking her, I walk the crew to the door. Once they leave, I briefly scan the house once again making sure nothing is left, and head out, locking all the doors. Before heading back to the station, I gave the key back to the neighbor. Her reaction to the burglary, and the dog dying was slightly entertaining, but as soon as she takes a breath from talking, I excuse myself.

There is literally nothing I want more than to get a coffee right now or go to bed. I like the sleep idea better.

"Good morning Officer Sousa. You're here early." Chief Kaiser greets me as I walk through the door to find Officer Perez.

I take a quick sip of the coffee I stopped to get before explaining to him the burglary situation that I had taken care of, leading me to stay on duty for several hours longer than I had expected.

Understanding, he continues, "Ah I see. Well, that's quite unfortunate. I do hope that you and Officer Perez will resolve this matter. Now onto lighter matters, my wife would like to know if you will be attending our Christmas party on the twenty-first?"

I like this change in topic because I'm too tired to try and recall what happened word for word. "Yes, I do believe that I will be going to the party. However, on the invitation, it does say that we are allowed to bring a significant other, would I be allowed to bring my roommate Kehlani?"

"Kehlani? Theo and Kayden's friend?" *Ah yes, those insufferable friends of Kiki's. I nearly forgot he's their father.*

Plastering a smile on my face, I reply, "Yes. I was planning on bringing her as my plus one. If it's too much, I don't mind not bringing her."

"Oh of course it's not too much. Ariel would love to see Kehlani again, and so would Theo." He says winking. *Ah yes, how could I forget that they're in a very interesting position right now? Can you hear my sarcasm?*

Thanking him, I dismiss myself, wanting to find Officer Perez, so that we can finish the draft of the report as fast as humanly possible. Once I find him, we both begin filling out our reports only speaking if we need to correct each other or have a question. Once a rough draft has been formed, we agree to edit the reports in two days when we return to work. I run out of there as fast as I can, quickly

7

clocking out wanting to get home before the caffeine wears off.

Chapter 2

"Honey! I'm home!" I yell as I take off my shoes when I get home.

After hearing some shuffling, my best friend yells back, "Welcome home darling! You're late." She walks out of her room dressed, and ready for work. "You were supposed to be home hours ago, and you were supposed to make my breakfast today. I didn't wake up when I heard you banging around in the kitchen. Now, I'm late and hungry." Kehlani dramatically pouts as she tries to get all her things for work.

All I can do is roll my eyes tiredly, "I'm so sorry Princess Kiki, that I work a job where anything can happen, and when a crime happens, I have to work overtime. It's definitely not like you could stop by and go get a quick breakfast before work since it's a Friday morning and everyone's more lenient at your school."

Kehlani just laughs at the sarcasm dripping from my voice. "Okay, Ms. Grumpy Pants. I can see you're tired. I need to go to work now, and when I get back, I pray that you've gone to bed and slept a bit so you can tell me what happened. And maybe you will go with me to Bible study with Ariel around six?" she asks me hopefully, knowing full well that I'm not going.

I just look at her, tired and annoyed, "No. I've told

9

you and Mrs. Kaiser many times, I'm not interested in that absurd God stuff that people use as an excuse for everything wrong with the world."

Kehlani just sighs, "Yeah. I know your stance on that. I just hoped that you would change your mind or something. Anyway, I'm going to head out now. Bye!"

Once the door closes, I look at the clock and notice that it's already eight a.m. *Finally, Sleep.* I practically run into my bathroom to take a quick shower and brush my teeth. Honestly, I have never been so happy to see my bed. Usually, it takes me a while to go to bed, especially after I've had to deal with some sort of arrest, but this time, sleep overcomes me within minutes.

Ring. Ring. Ring. As I slowly open my eyes, my brain starts to register that someone is calling me. *Who is calling me right now? And do they want to get hurt?* Groaning, I pull myself out of bed and check the caller I.D.

"What do you want?" I grumble when I pick up.

His annoyingly amused voice speaks up, "Well hello to you too. Aren't you a sweetheart this afternoon? Rough morning?"

"Kayden. You've just woken me up from the sleep that I've been needing for the past couple of weeks. What do you think?"

"I think you should sleep earlier than considering it's four p.m. but that could just be me, my dear."

Growling, I answer, "Two things. One, never say something like that again especially when you know as well as anyone that I have to stay out late occasionally due to calls. Two, don't do pet names. We're barely friends, and the only two reasons I tolerate you are because your father is my boss and because Kehlani would kill me if I kill you out of

10

annoyance. And calling me 'my dear' is weird even for you. Now, what do you want?"

His voice softens from the teasing tone it had before, "Oh. I'm sorry, I didn't realize that you were even working that late this morning. My mom said that you'd gotten off at two this morning, and it's four p.m. now. Back to the point though, my mom wants to know if you're going to the party on Sunday night, and if you're bringing a guest. Oh and to remind you it's a formal event"

Is it bad that I feel a little guilty shutting him down like that? Pushing down that thought instantly, I answer, "Yeah, I'll be there. I'm bringing Kehlani as my guest if she can make it." I pause before asking, "Why didn't your mom call me instead? Or ask your dad since he already asked me earlier this morning?"

I could picture him shrugging through the phone, "She was going to, but I offered to call as an excuse to talk to you, sweetheart. My dad, I guess, didn't get the chance to tell her you already said you'll be there." I can hear him smirking, and it only makes my already shortening temper shorter.

Using the sweetest voice I could muster I say, "Never. And I mean never call me sweetheart. We're not friends like that. Calling me sweetheart would also imply that I'm kind, and I am the furthest thing from the kind you can get without committing a crime."

"Okay, so sweetheart is definitely a no, but what about—"

I quickly interrupt him, done with his pestering, "No. Just no. Goodbye." With that, I hang up.

Sitting on my bed in silence, replaying what just happened only to realize that I was wide awake, and would have no chance of going back to bed. After taking a second to recover from that sad thought, I pop up out of my bed to go to my closet and see if there's anything I can salvage to wear to the Christmas Party. When I find nothing, my first thought is to just not go, but when the dramaticism calms down, I walk over to Kehlani's room knowing she probably has a dress I could wear.

As I look through the numerous formal dresses, a loud voice calls out from outside the room, "You better be awake Ria! I bring you food, and the least you can d do is be awake to eat it!"

Rolling my eyes, I walk out of her room saying, "Calm down Kiki, I'm awake. I'm in your room looking through your closet for a dress. Also thanks for the food. I kind of need it!" The sight of a fast food bag on the table has never looked so good.

I grab the bag of food and start eating, only to pause when I notice the suspicious grin on Kehlani's face, "Why are you looking at me like that?"

"Would you like to tell me why you were in my room looking through my closet? You know since you insist that my style is too *'frilly and formal'*"

Rolling my eyes, I retort, "You are so dramatic. Well, there's a Christmas party I was invited to by the Kaisers on the twenty-first, don't give me that look, and it's formal. Oh and since Theo hasn't mentioned it to you, you're my plus one. I don't care what you say, you're not getting out of it."

Her face lights up, and she starts rambling, "OH! I get to dress you and me up for a formal party. I'm so excited! Now you have hazel green eyes, so maybe you should wear a green dress. Or maybe a red one because it's Christmas, and it matches your skin tone. Oh and makeup!"

I'm now regretting even mentioning the party to her, "Please don't go crazy. I'd like to still live after this party to see my family for Christmas."

Kehlani just doesn't stop, and in an attempt to get her to do so, I yell, "Kehlani! Yes, you can do all that. We have the rest of the weekend to plan." *Hold up, why'd she stop by at home?* "Also, aren't you going to be late for your Bible study? Why did you bring me food when you usually go straight to your church?"

Her face forms into one of guilt, which only makes my guess seems likely to be correct, "Uh yes, I will be a little late, but I was hoping a little bit of food would convince you to maybe go with me to Bible study. Please? Just try it. They asked us to invite people to the service today, and I think you'll like it, and it's only girls tonight."

"Kehlani, I don't know why you keep trying, but it's just not happening. No matter how many times you ask me, I don't think I'll want to go anytime soon. I also had a stupidly long shift earlier, I'm not interested in spending time entertaining Jesus-obsessed people. No offense."

The disappointment is evident on her face, but frankly, I don't know why she keeps trying. "None taken. I will get you to come with me one day though. I will be back in about an hour or so, and when I get back, we are looking through dresses."

Nodding, I let her go and return to my food.

While I'm finishing up, my phone rings again, and when I check my phone, my mood brightens. "Hey, Damien. How are you?"

"Hey Julie, I'm good. I was just calling to check up on you. It's been a second." My best friend says.

"It's definitely been too long. We should go get dinner sometime soon." When he agrees, I launch into a summary of my long couple of weeks, and we both talk about plans for Christmas.

An hour later, my phone rings, and when I check it, the message is from Kehlani, reminding me that I will become a life-sized doll soon. Hearing me groan, Damien asks, "What happened?"

"Nothing, I'm being slightly dramatic. Kehlani is coming back home, and we're going to the Kaisers' Christmas

13

party on Sunday. It's also a formal party, so she's looking forward to experimenting with makeup and dresses on me later." I laugh out loud as I read Kiki's messages threatening me to stay awake.

A light chuckle comes from the phone, "Oh? Is Kehlani your plus one?"

"Yeah. Why?"

"I was just wondering. But on the bright side, I'm also going to the party since somehow, my mom got invited too. That's good news for me that you're going."

I just nod and continue talking about the party until he gets a call from someone else, and has to go. Lucky for me though, Kehlani gets back about three minutes later.

Once she's eaten a bit, and changed into more comfortable clothes, I'm immediately whisked away to start the long process of finding a dress, shoes, accessories, make-up styles, and hairstyles.

Chapter 3

"*M*aybe you were right." I sigh reluctantly, avoiding having to look at Kehlani through the mirror. I don't need to see the triumphant look on her face.

Looking at myself, I'm a little surprised, because looking back at me is a gorgeous woman in a red spaghetti strap dress that hung loosely on my body with a slit starting from the top of her knee. My normally wavy hair is straightened. While I still look like me, my makeup had a light peach smokey eye with eyeliner that drew attention to my hazel eyes. My lips were the same cherry red color as my dress. The blush on my cheeks was also a similar color. A very big contrast to my usual rushed mascara, and concealer. Same with my outfit. Usually, I just throw on whatever baggy clothing I have in my closet, or my work clothes, but after this, I won't mind occasionally dressing up.

Kehlani continues smiling as she assesses my look through the mirror, "I'm usually right when it comes to these types of things," she winks.

This girl is wearing a green, formal, floor-length, spaghetti strap maxi dress with a straight neckline. Her eye makeup consists of mascara, gold eyeshadow with winged green liner, and the liner leading under her waterline. To top off her look, her lips and blush were a matching nude dusty pink color.

Truthfully, I admire Kehlani for the effort she puts into her style and getting ready to go out.

"Okay. We should probably get going. I'm like eighty percent sure we're late." When I check the clock, my suspicions are confirmed, "Yep. We are at least fifteen minutes late, and I told Damien I'd meet him outside the house. Let's move."

Kehlani freezes, "Damien's going?" When I nod she continues, "Well, I hope for all our sakes, all the boys behave. But yeah let's move. Kayden, Theo, and Ashton are also waiting outside for us."

Oh yeah, we should go. The passive aggressiveness will be unbearable to deal with if we get there too late.

With a grimace, I quickly walk out the door with my best friend hot on my heels. We rush to get to the Kaisers' house, and as we pull in, I see the large white house. "Geez. I always forget that they're loaded. Must be nice." I comment.

As soon as Kehlani parks the car, we rush out of the car in search of our friends who have hopefully remained civil with one another in the time it takes us to get there. When we get to the door, we catch sight of the four guys standing on the porch with a smile. Relief fills me, and I greet each guy with a handshake and a smile.

Damien gives me a hug when we arrive. As he checks out my outfit, he says, "Hey Julie, I'm glad you're going to be here with me. That dress looks amazing on you." He fakes whistles, "You look hot."

Before I can answer, one of the other three guys yells out, "Hot is a temperature, not an adjective to describe someone with," causing all of us to laugh.

Turning around, I see Theo grinning, so I reply, "You are absolutely ridiculous. You know that he was just saying I look nice." Turning back to Damien I ask, "When are you going to give up calling me Julie? That's not my first name, nor does anyone call me by my middle name. It's not even my middle name. It's a nickname for my middle name"

Damien just shrugs and answers, "I've called you Julie since college. What's the point in stopping? Plus it's funny to see you get mad." The both of us then decide that we're too cold to stay outside and walk inside leaving Kehlani and the others outside.

Once we get inside the house, both Mr. and Mrs. Kaiser instantly bombard us with greetings and cheek kisses. When Mrs. Kaiser finally finishes fussing over my dress and make-up, the others walk in, and the cycle starts over again. I do get to laugh when she starts admonishing Kayden and Theo for having messed up their hair and suits before the first hour of the party has even finished. They both apologize like little boys, and it's hilarious.

"Theodore and Kayden! There is no way you're arm wrestling in the middle of a *formal* party right now. I swear, sometimes hanging out with you two is like babysitting a couple of children. You guys are twenty-five and twenty-six and acting like seven-year-old children for goodness sake." Kehlani reprimands, exasperated by the restless men she calls her friends. I, on the other hand, just laugh silently.

Bored, I scan the room looking for Damien, and when I catch him talking to a couple, I walk over to ask Ashton, "Who are those people Damien is talking to? I don't think I recognize either of them from the station."

He pauses for a moment trying to remember, "I could be wrong, but I believe that those are the De Lucas. I'm actually quite surprised they were invited, as I think there are rumors that they despise the current government and law enforcement we have right now. Although I won't be surprised if Mr. and Mrs. Kaiser invite the De Lucas to convince them to go to church with them."

I let out an unladylike snort, "You people confuse me so much. I could never understand why you willingly socialize and invite people to a party who are very vocal about the fact that they dislike you. And please don't give me any of the 'Jesus loves them, so I will love them too' crap because I don't buy it for a second."

Ashton gives me a pointed look, "Fine. Then I won't say that, but if you already know the answer, then why would you still ask?" He then walks away to join Kehlani who has given up trying to get Theo to stop messing around after Kayden apparently had won, and left to get a drink.

A deep voice speaks from behind me, slightly startling me, "I heard what you said, and Ria, why don't you just come to church one Sunday? It never hurts to just try and go to see what we've been talking about all this time. You seem to have questions anyway."

I snort again, as I watch him lean against the couch. *The ignorance of this man.* "No. I'm not going, because what's the point? For me to go and hear about how there's supposedly this higher being that loves and created me, but somehow lets me live and witness just how cruel and relentless this world is? To witness poverty, struggle, and the pain of others? I understand that many of the officers at my station, including your father, are Christians. While I respect your father, I cannot and will never understand how he can follow Christianity. How can you believe in a God who is good and loving yet allows children, freaking children, to suffer out in the streets? There's just too big of a contradiction."

Kayden looks anything but insulted. He looks amused which annoys me more than I'd like to admit. "You'd be surprised how many of your questions and confusion could be answered just by attending a study whether it be a service or the women's Bible study.

He shrugs, "While I'd love to answer your questions, sweetheart, you seem to be in a place where no matter what I say, you'll argue. You're going to think anything I say is nonsense and made up, which is why I suggest going to church on a Sunday or Wednesday, or at least Friday for Bible study with Kehlani. I won't force you to do anything since ultimately that's your choice, but you know my opinion." With that, he just casually stands up straight and walks off to go find his parents, leaving me unsure of how I would've responded to him.

What difference does it make if he explains it to me versus if a pastor explains it to me? And why did he walk away? Usually, people are so determined to start a fight and try and strong-arm me into believing in their crap.

As I'm deep in my thoughts, a sweet voice snaps me out of it, "Adria! Hi! It's been so long. It's good to see you. I was hoping that you'd show up and that my brothers hadn't scared you and Kehlani off."

When I catch sight of Brooklyn, she starts laughing, "You look puzzled and annoyed at the same time. Which one of my brothers did you just talk to? Theo with his antics or Kayden and his weird riddle-like ways of explaining things?"

I just shake my head, "I didn't realize my confusion was so evident. To answer your question it was Kayden. I'm not sure what just happened, but that's irrelevant right now. Look at you! It seems like you've discovered yourself these first couple months at college."

Brooklyn giggles, "Absolutely. It's been amazing living at CLU. I'm mostly glad that they require all sophomores to still live in dorms for their second year. Don't tell Kayden or Theo but I'm glad that I'm not home so they're not breathing down my neck. Somedays I feel like they're more protective than my parents are, and that's saying something. My dad's a police officer for goodness' sake."

"That sounds exactly like them." I roll my eyes, chuckling, "You're an education major right?"

"Yeah, I'm going into education," she agrees, "I'm honestly enjoying it. It's great learning at a Christian school where the professors and students share similar worldviews to mine. Especially when I find a cute guy who shares my worldview." Brooklyn just winks leaving me laughing.

"Look for that special guy now. It'll get a lot harder after college, but focus on your studies. I won't tell your brothers that this is your current plan. Heaven knows they will show up at your school to make sure that whoever you're hanging out with is acceptable by their standards."

"Oh my gosh, they totally would show up. Theo would mostly show up to watch Kayd lose it though if we're being honest." Brooklyn and I laugh at that, picturing the scene that would take place.

We talk for a couple more minutes, catching up before parting ways.

Chapter 4

$\mathcal{I}$ spend the next couple of minutes roaming the house looking for Kehlani. But while looking for her, I hear singing in the living room.

"Peace on earth
And mercy mild
God and sinner reconciled.
Joyful all ye nations rise."

I don't know why I stay, but listening to the lyrics and hearing the pure joy coming from those singing makes me want to stay and listen. *They really do just believe in this mystical unknown being, don't they? But how do they have such peace about it?*

"Julie, there you are. Julie. Julie." Damien says, shaking me out of my thoughts.

"Yeah? Sorry. I was distracted. Where were you?" I ask.

He shrugs and answers, "Talking to some people. Hopefully making some connections. To be honest, I didn't know that the Kaisers were so well acquainted with the people of the city."

"Yeah well, Chief Kaiser *is* the chief police officer of

21

Silver Valley, one of the bigger cities in California." I retort.

Damien rolls his eyes, "Well yeah, I know that. I just mean that they know these people well enough that they can invite them to their house for a party. Although granted, they invited my mother, so maybe it was just a really big party."

"Yeah, I don't think that it was a party for close friends. They invited nearly the whole police department. I mean, I guess when you have that much money from generational wealth, then why not," is all I can say. "How about we go find more food and hot chocolate?"

"Sure."

With that, we both walk away from the singing, and head somewhere else, and the questions I have fade to the back of my mind.

"Kehlani! I'm tired. Can we take off now?" I somewhat whine to Kehlani.

She rolls her eyes at me. *The audacity.* "Adria."

I look at her with an innocent look, "What?"

"You're whining like a child, but yeah it is kind of late. We can head home soon. Let's go say bye to everyone first."

I answer by saying, "I already said bye to the Kaisers, and Damien already left so I'm done–"

"Do we not get a goodbye, sweetheart?" Kayden interrupts, walking into the room with Theo and Ashton following right behind.

I look to Kehlani to help me get out of this because frankly, I don't have the energy to deal with three grown children. *That little. She left me to go say bye to everyone.*

"No. No, you do not. Well, maybe Ashton since he's tolerable. You and Theo do not though. I don't feel like dealing with you two tonight"

"Hey!" Theo exclaims, "What did I do? I'm not the one who bothers you."

I give him a pointed look, "You bother Kehlani, and you're Kayden's brother, that's saying enough."

"Cousin, thank you. We share twelve point five percent of our DNA." he returns.

"But you've lived together for the last fifteen years since you got adopted. The idiocy must have rubbed off on you."

Kayden interjects, "Both my degree in medicine and the MD on my scrubs would say otherwise to your claim that I'm an idiot."

Everyone just rolls their eyes, "Yes Kayden, we get it. You're trying to be a hero, and you went to school for six years. You may be book smart, but my comment on you being an idiot still stands."

He smiles smugly at me, only making my irritation grow, "Sure. We'll go with what you want to believe sweetheart."

He did not, I told him. Ugh, "How many times do I have to tell you not to call me by any nicknames? Especially not pet names. It's so weird when you call me sweetheart" I fake shudder

Kayden pretends to think for a second before answering," Uh, as many times as it takes to convince me that it doesn't fit you, and your reaction to me calling you sweetheart is no longer amusing."

"And that is enough of that, my children." Kehlani interrupts, saving Kayden from my anger. "Ria, we can go home now. And Kayd, stop antagonizing her. You're twenty-six, so act like it."

"Kehlani, we're not children. Don't treat us like we're in elementary school." I look at Kayden, "But you should listen to her when she says to start acting like a twenty-six-year-old."

23

"I do. It's just funny when you flip out because I'm teasing you." He throws back.

Kehlani steps between us, "And this is what I mean by you two arguing like children. I have an entire middle school class that bickers less than you two do."

We both roll our eyes, and everyone bursts into laughter.

Before leaving, I do say goodbye to everyone, yes, even Kayden and Theo. I'll take the high road just this once.

When we get in the car, it's decided that I'm driving home, and as I'm starting the car, Kehlani asks, "So, did you have fun?"

Pulling out of their street, I answer, "Yeah, I did. I got to hang out with Damien, and it's been a second since I've seen him. Oh, and I saw little Brooklyn. Well, I guess she's not so little anymore considering she's in her second year of college."

"Yeah. It was nice seeing everyone. I didn't really see you all night, but that explained where you were. Next time, you should come hang out with all of us, and yes I also mean outside of a party that you're stuck at."

I pause before answering so that Kehlani at least somewhat thinks that I'm considering going, "Maybe, but they aren't what I would consider friends. Heck, Kayden, Theo, and I don't even get along. And Ashton, sure he's nice, but I just don't click with him. Plus, there has not been a single conversation with them where they don't bring up their religion. I'd rather just not deal with that, no offense."

Kehlani only nods, and to be honest, I'd ask, but I'm too tired. This subject will come up again another day. The rest of the way home, I start tuning her out as Kehlani keeps talking about something I don't really catch.

"Good morning Officer Sousa." Officer Perez greets me when I walk through the door Monday morning.

Putting on a fake smile that should honestly be illegal for seven in the morning, I return, "Likewise to you, Officer Perez. Now we need to quickly work on our reports before I have to leave for a presentation at a local school."

Agreeing, we both quickly work on the reports and revise each other's work before I leave to head to the school.

To be completely honest, I don't really know what to expect when I get there and do the presentation. Being a police officer induced? some mixed reactions to the people who live in the city, and children absorb the information given to them by their parents, so I'm not too sure what reaction I'll be met with when I arrive.

When I arrive, I walk into the office to check in. Once my I.D. has been checked, I am led to the auditorium by the school principal. "So, all you have to do is give your presentation to the kids once I call you up, and then after, walk around to the lower grade classes and answer any questions. If you have time, I'm sure some of the kids would love it if you could stay for their lunchtime. I know you're a busy woman, so if you can't stay that's completely okay." She explains as she walks me through the auditorium explaining where I will stand, and all the technicalities.

Once she finishes talking, I stand behind the stage to wait as the children file into the room. Rereading my notes only makes my mind wander to the different duties I will need to fulfill later. All I can do is hope that none of the children here will jeer, or act up.

Soon, the school principal comes back to tell me they are ready for me to come on. "Good morning, Silver Hills Elementary School. I'm Officer Adria Juliette Sousa, and today we're going to be talking about what police officers do for the city."

"Adria! Kayden, Ashton, Theo, and I are heading out to get dinner before everything closes for Christmas. Would you like to come with us?" Kehlani asks when I get home.

I groan, plopping down on the couch, "One, as much as I would love to hang out with you, I just spent the day dealing with kids who hated me today, so no. Two, you know as well as I do, if your friends are going, then I won't go. I might just stay home and watch a show or something."

"Ria! Come on. Please, it's before Christmas. I want to spend time with you. Theo and Kayd will behave." She tries to beg.

I roll my eyes, "Nice try, You're going with me to my house for Christmas. We'll be together for at least three days. Also, Kayden and Theo will never behave, that's their thing. Nice try, but no thank you.

"Fine. I don't have to leave for a little. Do you want to talk about your crappy day?" She asks, sitting down next to me on the couch.

I sigh, and fall over dramatically, "Yes. I spent the day with two types of kids. One-half of the kids tried to do anything to get their hands on a weapon, and the other half were scared out of their minds that I was going to hurt them. They spent the entire time hiding in a corner."

Kehlani's rubbing my back as I continue, "I got several angry messages from some of the teachers as well." I smile weakly and say sarcastically, "So today was great."

"I'm sorry that that was your day. It sounded terrible." My best friend says sympathetically. "I'll try and control my students if you're the one coming by my school. "I'm guessing then the teachers didn't try to calm down the ones scared of you if they were scared themselves."

I shake my head, "Yep. I get that there are officers

that go against the oath, and put people at risk, but not all of us are like that. I wish they would understand. It broke my heart when I saw the fear in some of those children's eyes. It also made not yelling at the kids trying to steal my taser easier." I half-heartedly joke at the end.

"I do hope that when they grow up, they will learn that not all officers are bad, and they have nothing to fear." I nod sadly, "Did any of the kids warm up to you as the day went on?"

I smile, "Actually yeah. There was this adorable little second-grade girl, and she ended up hanging out with me all during their lunch recess. She very shyly asked me a question during her class even though she was basically hiding during the presentation."

Kehlani tries to encourage me. "Look, I know those kids and some adults have some weird dislike of law enforcement, but you're doing an amazing thing serving all of us. They don't realize it, but you guys are the ones keeping us safe."

"Yeah, yeah, I know. Now, aren't you going to be late meeting your friends at the place you guys are heading to for dinner?"

Kehlani sighs, "It's fine. They're always late anyway. Are you sure you don't want to come with us? They won't mind. I need another girl to control them."

I give her a pointed look, "Nope. Not a chance. Nice try though. You want to be friends with them, you're stuck with them. I'm staying home."

She gets up, and groans, "Fine. I'll see you when I get home. Don't destroy the house."

I roll my eyes, "Says the walking human disaster. See you soon."

Chapter 5

"Kehlani! Are you coming with me or not? We need to leave now! Charlotte and Elianna better not kill me for being late, and if they do, then you're the one who's going to have to deal with them" I yell to my roommate waiting by the door with my bag.

Once I finish yelling, the rustling, and thumping increases for a second before my best friend finally exits her room with a freaking suitcase that's about to burst open. "I'm here. I'm here. My goodness, you are impatient, and you and I both know that if we're late, your sisters will only be mad at you. They love me too much to hurt me"

I scowl at her knowing that she is completely correct. "Whatever. We need to leave now before traffic gets bad." Nodding, she starts to drag her suitcase, following me outside the house to the car.

When we get there I put my bag in the backseat, and when I close the door, laughter bursts from my chest at the sight of Kehlani trying to put her suitcase in the trunk. "What on earth did you need to pack for a three-day stay at my mom's?" I'm doubled over with laughter at this point.

Kehlani rolls her eyes after she gets the suitcase in the trunk before answering, "Christmas presents obviously. I bought some things for your mom, and your sisters too."

"No presents for me?" I tease.

She shakes her head and smirks.

"Wow. I can really feel the love here. You know, sometimes I feel like you're only friends with me so that you can see my sisters and my mother." I complain.

Kehlani smiles, amusement filling her eyes, "It's possible. But the affection is mutual. I mean your mom and sisters love it whenever I go with you back to your house."

My eyes roll again before I climb into the driver's seat.

"I call aux!" Kehlani exclaims when she gets in the car, and I don't even bother trying to argue with her."

"Kehlani!" One of my twin sisters exclaims as she bolts out of the house the minute I park my car ready to jump my best friend.

A couple of seconds later, her identical twin walks out much calmer saying, "Elianna, let them get out of the car first for goodness sake."

Elianna just shrugs and waits for a second until Kehlani exits the car before jumping into her arms to hug her. *Well dang. I guess I know who Ellie likes more.*

Charlotte on the other hand walks up to me first and gives me a big hug. "Hey Ria! I missed you. I wish you come home more often and stay longer than a few days for Christmas." *I needed that hug from my little sister.*

After a couple of seconds, Elianna finally lets go of Kehlani and gives me a quick hug. I roll my eyes at my little sister, "Good to know who your favorite is when you've known me all fourteen years of your life."

Sheepishly she apologizes, "Sorry Ria, you know I love you too." We all laugh, "Anyways, Mom's waiting for y'all to get in the house with a nearly disgusting amount of

30

food and pastries waiting for you on the table."

"Alright people, let's get inside, and get ready for a hurricane of questions and hugs," I say as we walk towards the house.

As I expect, the minute we walk into the house, my mother bombards us with hugs and kisses, "My babies! How are you? You both look so skinny and tired that you need to rest and eat. Eat something I made, then take your bags up to Adria's room to settle in, and take a nap for a couple of hours."

Laughing, I tell my mom that we aren't tired nor malnourished. "Mom, it's a three-hour drive from Silver Valley to Roseburrough, we're okay."

"Ah yes well, driving can be exhausting with all these Christmas Eve idiots driving on the roads." Mom throws back.

Giving up, I decide to take Kehlani's and my bags upstairs and set up the extra bed. When I'm finished, I start to walk downstairs before pausing at the stairs. I don't really know why, but listening to my family laughing with my best friend makes me smile.

"You actually don't have a boyfriend?" I hear Elianna exclaim as I walk into the living room and take a seat next to Charlotte on the couch.

"I mean, no one's caught my interest, nor do I want to date right now." Kehlani lies straight through her teeth.

Raising my eyebrows at her, she rolls her eyes, so I know it's okay to say this next part, "No one that has caught your interest? Really? So sticking to Theo basically like glue all night at the Christmas party meant nothing?" Elianna and Charlotte's eyes go wide, "In fact, when I was invited to that party, Chief Kaiser asked me if my plus one would be you. And his comment after that was and I quote, 'Because Theo would love to see her.' Just saying."

My sisters then jump off the couch and jump on

31

Kehlani, grilling her on Theo while I stay there laughing. Kehlani just looks at me with a glare that says I'm going to pay for this later, but I can't bring myself to care. I just return her look with one of innocence.

Now that my sisters are distracted, my mom decides that it's my turn to get interrogated. "How are your cases doing? Have you had to do anything dangerous yet?"

I bite my lip, and consider lying to her, but decide against it, "Not yet, but I do have to be present for a demonstration slash protest soon, and you know how those can sometimes get out of hand, especially in Silver Valley."

My mom starts questioning me on what I will need to do, and the precautions that will be taken for both the protesters and for me. We continue talking for another hour or so before Kehlani and I start yawning. *Maybe a three-hour road trip does tire you out after.*

"I'm going to go to bed, I'm getting tired from the three-hour drive. Goodnight Mrs. Sousa, thank you for letting me stay here for Christmas. Night, El and Char." Kehlani then walks upstairs to get ready for bed.

I just roll my eyes, and say to my family, "She is so dramatic. She didn't even drive at all for the three hours here, I did. The girl sat in the car like a little passenger princess the whole time. She does have the right idea though, I'm going to go try and sleep now. Goodnight y'all." I give each of them a hug before running upstairs.

I run to the bathroom and quickly get ready for bed. When I'm finished, I walk into my room ready to crash. Kehlani is sitting on the pullout bed that I had set up for her deep in concentration. She was reading from a decently large-sized book with some highlighters, occasionally stopping to mark something on the page. Curious, I climb onto her bed, catching a sentence that was on the page.

"In Me, you may have peace. In the world you will have tribulation; but be of good cheer, I have overcome the

32

world."

"Adria. Adria. Hello? Are you there?" Kehlani is waving a hand in front of my face, bringing me out of my thoughts.

"Yeah. Sorry. What did you say?"

She nods and repeats herself, "I just asked if you were ready for me to turn off the lights. I'm done reading now."

I just nod and climb into my bed. We say goodnight, and she turns the lights off. Kehlani fell asleep quickly, but the words that I had seen on the page of her Bible kept me thinking. *Peace? How can a book promise someone peace? Especially now.*

I let myself rot in my thoughts, tossing and turning. When I check the clock, I realize it's already midnight and sigh, so I get up to go get some water. *"In the world, you will have tribulation, but be of good cheer, for I have overcome the world."* I just don't understand this line. I understand being content during a time of trial since it helps you grow as a person, but how could you be cheerful?

I scoff to myself, knowing Kehlani and Kayden, they would spout some crap about how Jesus saved them so they have all this joy. To me, that's absolute crap. Overcome the world? This world is ten times worse than what it had been twenty years ago. To say you have peace and joy going through the motions of life is incomprehensible.

As I'm going back upstairs, my mind is still running around like a hamster on a wheel, and truthfully, I don't know what to make of it. When I get back to my room, I climb over Kehlani, trying not to wake her up, and back into my bed.

I would ask her about all this, but I want an answer that's not influenced by someone who's part of the religion. As harsh as this may seem, Kehlani and Kayden have had it all, they both grew up with successful parents, they never struggled to go through school, and never struggled with poverty. After a while of tossing, turning, and thinking, around one or two in the morning, I finally fell asleep.

Knock. Knock. Knock. Knock. "Adria. Kehlani. Wake up. It's nearly ten a.m., and I need you two to be up. We're going to open presents downstairs," is the first thing I hear when I open my eyes the next day. I groan feeling like I have only just closed my eyes.

I roll out of bed and open the door to be met with my mom who is fully dressed and has a full face of makeup on. "I'm up Mom. Kehlani on the other hand, you're going to need to give her about another ten to fifteen minutes."

"Okay, that's fine. I do need to ask you a favor though. Can you wa—" she starts to ask.

I shake my head, "Absolutely not. They are terrors if you wake them up too early. Nope. I decided to work in Silver Valley just so I wouldn't have to deal with them when they wake up."

Mom just gives me a pointed look, and returns, "You were the exact same way when you were fourteen, and I had to wake you up every day. Go wake up your sisters, please. I'll be waiting downstairs for you all."

I can only groan before trying to wake Kehlani up when Mom leaves. "Kehlani, wake up." I try shaking her awake. "Please come with me to wake up the twins. If you do, they won't get as angry as they would if I wake them up."

Kehlani rolls towards me, keeping her eyes closed before mumbling, "It's too early, I'm not going to get up. Let me sleep. Go wake up your sisters, I'll get up when they're awake." With that, she turns around and falls back asleep.

Grumbling, I decide to walk into the den of lions.

34

Knock. Knock. Knock. I wait for a second, and when there's no answer, I carefully open the door, and say, "Charlie, Ellie, wake up, it's Christmas Day. Mom wants us to be downstairs soon."

Ellie moves around a bit before mumbling, "No. Get. out. It's Christmas break. Let. Me. Sleep." Charlie on the other hand is still dead asleep.

I roll my eyes, "Girls, get up. You need to get up before Mom kills all three of us for not waking up, and going downstairs. Get up, Kehlani is already waiting too."

Instead of getting up, and saying *"Oh okay my darling sister, I'll wake up."* Ellie says instead, "Get. OUT!" And then she has the audacity to throw a pillow at me.

"Elianna Morgan Sousa, you did not just throw a pillow at me in an attempt to go back to sleep." She just throws a stuffed animal at me. "That's it, get your butt up and out of bed. If you throw another thing at me, I will end you faster than you can say 'Merry Christmas'. Don't test my patience."

Elianna finally starts to get up, but Charlie's still sleeping like she's dead. I walk over to her, and shake her gently, "Charlie, I need you to get up, please." She's still not moving. If I didn't know my sister, one would assume that she was dead. "Charlie, wake up." I take her blanket off her, and she finally starts to stir. With that, I physically have to drag her out of bed.

"I'm up. I'm up." she groans. "Adria, I'm tired, let me sleep."

"For goodness sake, I'm not repeating this one more time, so both of you listen, and listen well. Get up now. Mom's waiting for us downstairs and wants us to get up. It's already ten, and no you can't go back to sleep." Ellie's already awake, but Charlie groans and lightly tosses something at me. *Oh my. They really don't like getting woken up. Even Charlie's acting like a freaking monster. What happened to my baby sisters?*

With that, I just leave the room, not wanting to have anything else thrown at me this morning. "When I get back with Kehlani, you both better be up, and ready to take a bunch of pictures. If you two aren't ready then it's not my problem."

Walking into my room, I'm hoping that my best friend isn't still sleeping, and thank goodness she wasn't. "Good. I'm glad you're awake. Although I'm still annoyed you left me to go into the den of lions by myself." I tease. "Teenagers are not easy to wake up. Were we like this when we were their age?"

Kehlani rolls her eyes, and answers, "I don't think so, but our parents would probably say otherwise." She pauses as she crawls out of bed, "How long do I have to get ready before your sisters run in here, or your mom asks us all to go down?"

"Good to know that you only listen to me when it's convenient for you. You have fifteen minutes before the girls come in, assuming they're only putting on a little makeup. You have twenty to thirty minutes before my mom comes bolting up here angry we're not down yet." I say as I run to the bathroom to put on my makeup.

Once I, along with Kehlani and the twins, are finished getting ready, we walk downstairs, to meet my mother. When we get down, we are ready to celebrate Christmas and hang out with each other for the day.

Chapter 6

"*D*o you guys actually have to leave today?" Charlie asks, giving me her best puppy dog eyes. If I'm being completely honest, if I didn't have to drive three hours today, and then work tomorrow, I might've given in, but unfortunately, that's not an option.

"Yes Charlie, unlike you, Ellie, and Kehlani, I have to work tomorrow," I say.

Ellie chimes in, "So then can Kehlani stay until winter break is over?"

Kehlani answers this time instead, "I have to get home too you know. I'd love to stay, but we only brought one car. How else would I get home if I didn't go with Ria?"

"Yeah. Yeah. We know. It was worth a shot though." Charlie replies.

Kehlani gives both Charlotte and Elianna a hug as I finish putting our bags and suitcases in the car. When I finish, the twins detach from Kehlani and jump on me instead. *When did they become so clingy? Not that I'm complaining, just confused.*

"I'll be back soon, or you guys could come visit us in Silver Valley soon. You guys will be busy for the rest of the break hanging out with your friends anyway." I say as I hug both my sisters tight.

Both of them nod, and my mom gives Kehlani and me a hug as well before we get into the car. As I'm climbing into the passenger seat of the car, she gives me the classic mom talk. 'Be safe, stay alert, I love you, etc...'

I tell my family I love them, and Kehlani says thank you, and we're off to head back home.

As my best friend drives, we talk for a bit, but eventually, both of us succumb to our thoughts. I went back to the words in Kehlani's Bible. For me, it's genuinely hard to grasp that someone could be so perfectly happy with their lives even if it's all falling apart.

> *"Brown guilty eyes and little white lies*
> *Yeah, I played dumb, but I always knew."*

The lyrics fill the car, and both Kehlani and I sit up straighter and sing along with the popular song.

> *"You betrayed me.*
> *And I know you'll never feel sorry,*
> *For the way I hurt, yeah."*

We're both laughing as we're singing, every previous doubt and concern I have gets pushed to the back of my mind.

> *"Don't you dare forget about the way*
> *You betrayed me.*
> *Cuz I know that you'll never feel sorry*
> *For the way I hurt, yeah."*

> *"Guess you didn't cheat,*
> *But you're still a traitor."*

The two of us giggle as the song ends. We sing a couple more songs before I get tired, and slowly start to nod

38

off.

During the next couple of weeks, I work my butt off since we were extremely short-staffed. Every day I come home so exhausted and fall asleep within five minutes of laying down on my bed.

Ring. Ring. Ring. I groan and slowly reach over to my dresser to grab my phone. *Who the heck is trying to wake me up at six in the freaking morning. I will actually hurt whoever is trying to make me get up early on the only day I've had off in the last ten days.*

"Hello, is this Officer Adria Sousa?" A female voice says over the phone when I answer.

Internally I groan, already knowing what's about to be said, "Yes, this is she. What is the reason for the call?"

"Yes well, I'm extremely sorry for having to ask this as I know this is your day off, but we're short one patrol for today, and we need you to be out on patrol by seven-thirty." The woman explains.

Muting myself, I whine to myself for a quick second before unmuting and replying, "Of course. I will be there as soon as possible, I've just woken up so I'll be there as soon as possible."

Once I've hung up the phone, I am already complaining, annoyed that my day off was canceled. *Oh well. I signed up for this when I went through the training.*

As quickly as I possibly can, I get ready for work, and rush out the door holding a bagel. *Alright, let's hurry. I know how badly the on-shift officers want to go home.* But as I'm starting the car, my phone rings three times. I quickly check my phone thinking it was either Kehlani or Damien, but it's not.

Kayden: Hey sweetheart, I was wondering if you wanted to come hang out with us today? Now don't lose your mind just yet and say no, hear me out. Kehlani and Theo are hanging out tonight, and we were wondering if you wanted to come hang out with us. Before you ask, Ashton isn't coming. I know you're not my biggest fan, but both Theo and I would love to get to know Kehlani's best friend. If you don't want to come then that's okay as well.

His text catches me off guard, so I decide to respond to the other two messages first. The first one was a message from Damien.

Damien: Hey Julie. I'm so sorry, but something came up, and I can't make it to the movie night we had planned for tomorrow. I'll try and call soon so we can figure out a day when we can hang out.

Me: Oh that's totally fine. I'm free tonight if that works out for you. I'm leaving right now for work, so I should be off of work by around five. If not then just let me know.

The last message is just one from Theo. It was basically a more annoying and threatening version of the text that Kayden had sent. I decide to ignore Theo and answer Kayden instead knowing that he would relay the message

40

I type out a message that says I would rather do anything else than hang out with him, but for some reason, I pause before sending the message. *Why do I hate him so much? He's been nothing but kind. Sure there's the occasional teasing, but nothing worse than any of my other friends.* The more I ponder why I've never given him the chance, the more I can't come up with a good excuse to be rude. Sighing, I send a different message.

> *Me: Hey Kayd, if you hate that nickname, then deal with it considering you still haven't listened to me. Please stop calling me sweetheart. I'm finding it very weird that you knew what I was going to ask, and you answered the questions. You also knew my first instinct was to say no, so for that, I'll give it a chance. I'll be there around five-thirty or later if Damien can't hang out tonight...*

Kayden*: Kehlani told me what to say to you so I can't take the credit. No, I will not stop calling you sweetheart. I still find it ironic. I have a surgery to observe/assist with today, and I get off around five. If you can go, I can pick you up if you want, and then you can just go home with Kehlani since she and Theo are going to the fair today. Let me know what the plan is.*

41

"I'm so sorry for the inconvenience. I will make sure that my daughter learns her lesson about dialing 911 for fun. Again my apologies." The frantic and embarrassed mother says to me after I'd shown up because of the call.

Not able to even be mad, I simply responded with, "It's alright ma'am just so long as she learns not to call us unless it's an emergency."

I turn to the little girl, and speak to her softening my tone, "How come you called 911?"

"I uh. I called because in school we learned that you would come with the sirens on if we called 911 and said someone was stealing something. I just wanted to see and hear the sirens." The girl mumbles as she plays with a doll in her hand.

As hard as I try, I can't be annoyed with the girl, after all, I was once her age too. "That's okay that you wanted to hear the sirens, but they're only for if people are in big danger. Next time if you want to hear the sirens, just sit outside on the porch and you'll probably hear a siren passing the street okay?"

She nods and apologizes again. As I'm leaving, her mother also apologizes, having calmed down from the embarrassment, promising to teach her daughter when it's appropriate to dial 911.

I wearily climb back into my car, exhausted from the several calls I have received. I am more than excited for my lunch break, so I head over to a diner, to order some food.

After ordering, I sit down to check my phone, and notice I have gotten a message from Damien.

Damien: I'm sorry, I can't do tonight. If you're not working late on the fourteenth, I'm free. Call me when you're on your lunch

42

break though, and we can talk
then to figure it out.

> *Me: Okay. Just give me a second,*
> *I need to go get my food, and let*
> *Kehlani know I can hang out with*
> *her tonight.*

Before I can send Kayden or Kehlani a text, the waitress brings my food, and it smells heavenly. As I'm eating, I send the text.

> *Me: Well, it looks like luck is on*
> *your side. I will be gracing you*
> *with my presence later today. Tell*
> *Kehlani and Theo. I'll be there*
> *around five, five–thirty ish, and*
> *you are not picking me up. I have*
> *a car. You don't need to play the*
> *gentleman.*

I then finally call Damien. We talk for about a half-hour, discussing the movie we're going to watch in three days, and where we will go to eat. As he's telling me about a restaurant he wants to try, my phone buzzes, letting me know I have a notification.

When Damien finishes his sentence, I say, "Hang on, I just got a message."

> *Kayden: Don't be ridiculous and*
> *start putting words in my mouth.*
> *I'm going to pick you up since*
> *your house is on the way from*
> *the hospital back home. It'd be*
> *pointless, and you'd be wasting*
> *gas. I'll see you at five-thirty. Oh, I*

also told Theo and Kehlani you're coming. Theo didn't answer, but Kehlani says he nearly went into cardiac arrest when he heard you were coming.

> **Me**: *And somehow women are the dramatic ones. Fine, you can take me, but no calling me any nicknames on the ride to your house. I'll see you at five-thirty. If you're late, I'm leaving by myself.*

Kayden: *I'll try but no promises.*

I roll my eyes, and as I do, Damien gets impatient waiting for me to respond, and asks, "Who are you texting, Julie?"

Annoyed, I say, "Damien Mariani, stop calling me Julie. Juliette is my middle name, and nobody calls me by my middle name for goodness sake." I purposefully avoid answering the 'Who are you texting?' question, knowing that if I told him the truth, he would go on and on about how ridiculous Kehlani's friends act, and although I agree with him, neither of us has the time for that. I also just don't have the energy to sit through him blabbering and complaining.

"Fine, I'll stop. No, not really, I'm still calling you Julie. It makes you sound so much older than you are." He laughs as I groan in defeat.

Noticing that my lunch break should've been over about five minutes ago, I tell him, "Okay, I have to go now. I'll see you in a couple of days. Bye, bestie-bear." I then hang up on him as he protests the nickname.

Chapter 7

Crap. It's already almost five. I need to get ready. My throat is dry after waking up from my nap, so I quickly run to the kitchen and grab some water. As I'm drinking, my phone rings again, and I'm really hoping it's not Kayden telling me he's going to be early. Thankfully, it's not.

Kehlani: Adria, I know you're awake. I saw you in the security camera. Kayden said you're going out with us today. Don't eat dinner yet, we're going to go out and get food.

> *Me: Are you stalking me? I literally just got out of bed from a nap two minutes ago. By the way, Kayden insisted on driving, so if either of us ends up dead, you are responsible.*

Kehlani: No, I am not stalking you, I was checking the cameras because I left my sweater and lipstick at home. Oh, Theo also says he's annoyed that you didn't answer his invitation, but you answered Kayden's.

>*Me: Oh that little brat... I ignored him because he threatened me, and also Kayden would've relayed the message, and he clearly did.*

Kehlani: *Well, he never got Kayden's message, since the idiot left his phone at home. Anyway, we're still at the fair, and I found a spot where there's internet. We're about to leave, so we're going to be late. Kayd's going to bring you to his and Theo's house. We're going to watch a movie and order food. If I don't respond, it's because your message didn't go through.*

>*Me: Okay, see you later.*

Looking up at the clock, I realize that I should start changing, and fixing my makeup, and my hair. I quickly put my hair in a messy bun, pulling out the front pieces before cleaning up my under eyes of mascara. When I check my closet, I throw on light blue baggy jeans and a white tank top.

As I'm grabbing the things Kehlani left at home, the doorbell rings. "Hold on, I'm grabbing a jacket!" I call out as I put on an oversized navy blue bomber jacket

"Hey Adria, do you need help?" Kayden greets me as I put my shoes on.

"I'm good, thanks. It's just some of Kehlani's things, and my bag."

"Not to overstep, but are you sure you won't be cold wearing a tank top and a thin jacket?" He asks.

I roll my eyes at the audacity, "Oh are you sure you're

worried for my health, or are you misogynistic and scared you and Theo will be distracted by my shoulders showing all night."

"Oh my goodness, you're so right. How will I ever be able to focus? Oh, and you're wearing ripped jeans." he gasps dramatically, and continues teasing, "So much skin, how will I survive?"

"You are infuriating. Don't judge my clothing taste Mr. 'I look like my mother has dressed me for church'. Didn't you come from surgery today? How are you even wearing a white knitted Ralph Lauren sweater?" Actually, I am very curious.

He looks at me amused, "You do realize that in surgery we were scrubs right… This is just something I wore once I changed out of scrubs that were uh… dirty. Same with the jeans."

Well now I feel stupid, so I scoff, lock the door behind me, and storm off.

Kayden makes it worse by laughing. "Sweetheart, I parked on the street, and you don't know which car is mine." He calls out behind me.

"Keep this up, and I will walk back into that house." I threaten.

He finally stops laughing and apologizes. "Okay. Okay. I'm sorry." He then leads me to his car.

Once we get into his car, an awkward silence fills the car, so I turn on the radio in hopes of killing the awkwardness.

Kayden is the first one to break the silence, "You're quiet. Nervous being in the same car as me sweetheart?"

That is my breaking point, "Pull over. I'm getting out. I'm not dealing with you calling me nicknames. We agreed that you would do none of this."

The car doors lock and Kayden rolls his eyes, "It's just a nickname. I'm sorry it was a reflex. You agreed to hang out with Kehlani and Theo too, not just me, so you can't just bail. Also, the doors are locked." At the last sentence, he smiles innocently. We then bicker for the rest of the ride to his house.

When we walk into his house my eyesight is filled with whites and different shades of gray. "For the love of everything, your house is as pretentious as you are."

Confusion crosses Kayden's face, "You're upset that my house is clean, and doesn't smell weird? Is this normal? Most women like it when houses are clean."

I raise my eyebrows. "Most women? One, you're borderline being stereotypical. Two, how many women do you bring around to your house?"

"Jealous are we?" I glare at him and he sighs before saying, "Fine. Most people. I still don't get why you're annoyed."

"It's not the fact it's clean, *Kayden*, more so the fact it looks like an open house. There's one picture hung up, and I'm pretty sure it's your family portrait. That's what I mean by pretentious." I snort.

Understanding crosses his face, but he's still calm which kind of impresses me, "Theo and I are never home. If we aren't at work, then we're at church. If we aren't at either of those places we're probably out with friends or family. Decorating was just never important, especially when all I want to do is sleep after a twelve-hour shift, or being on call for a day."

He makes sense, and I hate it. I sit down on the couch and watch as he walks around the house grabbing food, and snacks for us to eat.

Kayden walks away, opens a door, and yells, "I'm getting some drinks from the garage. What kind do you want?"

Still annoyed with him, I yell back, "Nothing! Who wants a lukewarm drink that's been sitting in a garage for God knows how long?"

"You little brat…" I can hear the amusement in Kayden's voice, "We have a fridge just for drinks in here for goodness sake. And you say Theo and I are the spoiled ones, my goodness."

"Ugh, whatever. Can I have a Dr. Pepper if you have some?" I relent, refusing to give him the satisfaction that he made sense.

Kayden walks out from the garage, and back to the living room, "No, you may not. You've insulted me and my pride enough today." He grins as he places the drinks he got out on the table. I notice the Dr. Pepper and grab it, rolling my eyes at his antics.

"Oh shut up. Thanks for the drink. Now where is my best friend? She said she'd be here at the latest at six. It's almost six." I ask as I send Kehlani a message asking where she is.

Kayden gives me a pointed look, "It's not six yet though…" I ignore that comment. "I can't ask Theo, he left his phone here. If they're really late though, your message wouldn't go through since they'd be driving out of the middle of nowhere."

Sighing, I send Kehlani another message, telling her to text me when she receives it. Kayden and I then default to having a light conversation, occasionally getting distracted by the TV show he put on.

After around fifteen minutes, my phone starts ringing. *I swear if that's not Keh— oh it's the Roseburrough Police Department…* "Hey Kayden, I need to take this phone call. Can I go into one of the rooms to answer it?" He nods and leads me to what I assume is either his room or the guest room.

I pick up the phone, hoping it's nothing bad, "Hello?"

"Hello, this is the Roseburrough Police Department. May we speak to Miss Adria Sousa?"

"Yes, this is she. How may I help you?"

49

"I'm sorry to be the one to deliver this news," my heart sinks. *My family.* I pace around the room, "We received a call from one of your younger sisters, and I regret to inform you that your mother has passed away. We do not yet know the cause of her death, but you were the listed emergency call for both your mother and your sisters." The world just stops, and I freeze.

"Hello? Ma'am?"

I shake myself out of my shock, sinking to the floor. "Hi, sorry. I'm still here. I will be there as soon as possible. I live around three hours away though, so it will be a while."

"Okay, well your sisters will be staying at a friend's house, and their friend's mother has just picked them up. The girls should give you the address. Your mother's body is currently at St. Mary's Hospital, where they are doing tests to find the cause of death." The caller explains.

My brain has gone blank, and although I can hear what the lady is saying, I can't bring myself to speak.

Knock. Knock. "Adria? Is everything okay?" Kayden asks from outside the door. I try to tell him I'm fine, but no words come out. "Hello? Are you okay?" When I don't answer a second time, he opens the door slowly, "Adria?" He walks in and sits next to me. After a moment, he either sees my phone is still on or hears the caller still speaking. Kayden then picks up the phone, listening to all the instructions that are being given before hanging up.

I'm not sure why he asks, considering he's probably figured it out, but he does anyway, "What did she call for?"

My voice starts shaking, "M...my...mom. She's dead. My sisters found her body at home."

Kayden envelops me in a hug, the clean and strong scent of his cologne starting to bring me out of my shock. He asks, "Do you need anything?"

My brain finally starts functioning, and we break out of the hug. "I need Kehlani right now. I need her to drive me to Roseburrough. I need to go pick up my sisters, or at least sort out who their guardian will be now."

Kayden's face sinks and he says, "Before I walked in here, I knew something was wrong so I texted Kehlani to see where she and Theo were, and the message never went through. They're still in the desert, and at least forty-five minutes away."

I start to panic, "Okay. Okay. I'll just take an Uber, or a cab, or something." I then get up and start rushing to the door.

As I'm about to open the door, Kayden grabs my arm and says, "Adria, that's ridiculous. Roseburrough is three hours away. The price of that trip would be beyond expensive. And what happens if you have to bring your sisters back to Silver Valley? I'll take you."

The surprise is probably evident on my face, "You? Why would you take me to Roseburrough? It's a six-hour round trip, and it's already past six p.m. We wouldn't get there until nine at the earliest. I say this in the most respectful way possible as well, but we're not even friends. Why would you do this for me?"

"Well for one, it's late, and I don't want to inconvenience a driver who would have to drive six hours tonight. I can stay at a hotel out there. Two, I have the weekend off, and I want to help you. Three, I want us to be friends. And four, stop arguing with me, we're wasting time. Let's go." He says as if this is the most casual thing he's ever said.

Unfortunately, he's right, "Okay, fine. You can take me to Roseburrough. We should find a way to let our friends know where we're going though." He agrees, so we quickly leave a note on the table for Theo and Kehlani, if they ever make it back here, and take off.

Chapter 8

The silence between us as we walk back to Kayden's car is loud, and extremely awkward. Tears begin pooling in my eyes, so I look down in an attempt to keep my crying inconspicuous. When we get to the car, Kayden opens the door for me. Once I'm in the car, he walks over to his door, gets in, and asks me for the address. Once it's on the map, he backs out and starts driving us.

Why me? What happened to Mom? I saw her a couple of weeks ago and called her yesterday. She seemed completely fine.

Where are Ellie and Charlie going to go? And how are they going to be mentally after finding their mother dead when they got home? What's going to happen to our house? I can't take care of the girls, we don't have space. What am I going to do?

My mind goes wild following different paths as Kayden continues driving. It feels like my whole world is falling apart, and I don't know how to stop it. My head falls into my legs as I curl up into a ball ignoring the precautions I'd learned about in training.

After a couple of minutes, I feel the car stop, so I immediately look up, confused. We are at a coffee shop drive-thru.

53

Pulling up to the speaker, Kayden orders an iced mocha latte, a chocolate croissant, and a chocolate chip muffin.

When we get to the window, he takes the items he ordered and hands them to me while he pays. After paying, Kayden just starts driving again. *Am I just supposed to hold the food and coffee?*

About ten minutes later I speak up and ask, "Do you want me to hold all this? Or can I put the drink in the cup holder, and the food on the side or something?"

"You can do whatever you want with the coffee and the food. It's all for you, considering you haven't eaten dinner yet. Plus you'll probably need the coffee if you're going to deal with everything later, especially your sisters who may not be in a good mental state." Kayden answers simply as if he didn't just do one of the nicest things anyone's ever done for me.

I freeze a bit before turning to him incredulously, "Are you joking?" When he shakes his head, I continue, "Why did you get me coffee and food? You're already driving me three hours for what? To watch my sisters and I probably have a mental breakdown? Why are you being so nice to me? What do you want from me? We're not friends, and it's not like I'm nice to you either."

Kayden doesn't even look at me, instead keeping his eyes on the road. "I got you coffee and food because like I already said, you haven't eaten, and that would've caught up to you later tonight if you didn't eat. I'm driving you because you're in no mental state to drive three hours, paying for a cab fare is expensive and stupid if I'm available and have the resources and time to drive you, and I'm not going to make you suffer by waiting for Kehlani."

He continues, "Again about the part about friends, I want to be your friend. And no, I want nothing from being friends with you, and you owe me nothing for driving you,

54

I'm simply here to help."

I fidget in my seat, still confused as he pauses seemingly hesitant before saying, "Look, I know you're not Christian, and you're probably going to call this nonsense but hear me out. The Bible says in Proverbs chapter seventeen, verse seventeen, 'A friend loves at all times, and a brother is born for adversity.'

I open my mouth to argue, but he stops me, "Don't even start by saying I'm telling you this so you'll become a Christian, I'm not. I'm telling you this because these are my beliefs, and I'm using the verse to back up and explain my actions."

I just nodded and said, "Okay. I suppose it makes sense."

While he's driving, my mind cannot stay out of the twists and turns of trying to figure out what happens next. Thoughts are rushing all around my mind trying to cope not just with my mother's death, but also with the future of my sisters.

I'm never going to get to say goodbye to Mom ever again... She's really gone. I'm never going to get to see her again. Those couple phrases continue to repeat in my head like a mantra trying to kill me. Tears start to fill my eyes, and my breaths starts to quicken and become shallow. The tears I am trying to hold in are flowing as it gets hard to breathe. I can't see anything through my tears, and I can no longer hear the car's engine. *Breathe. Breathe. Breathe. Freaking breathe!*

"Hey. Hey. Hey. Can you hear me?" Kayden's soft voice asks, sounding far away. I barely nod, still unable to see through my tears or calm my breathing.

"You're okay Adria, just listen to my voice. I parked the car, you're okay. Focus on my voice." He grabs my hand, and continues, "Okay, I want you to tell me five things that you can see right now."

55

I try looking around, but everything's fuzzy. I try looking closer to me and say, my voice shaking, "I…I…can s…see you. I…c…can see th…the road." Tears fill my eyes again, and I start shaking and sobbing. *Why can't I calm down for goodness sake? This is ridiculous.*

"Come on, three more things. You can do it." Kayden encourages.

"There's th…the coffee. Th…the steering wheel. My ja…jacket." *I can't do this.*

Kayden nods and says, "What are four things you can hear?"

Why can't I focus? I close my eyes, trying to listen, "I can h…hear your voice. I can hear the cars p…passing by. There's the s…sound of my voice. A…and your breathing."

"Amazing, sweetheart. One more time okay? What are three things you can feel right now?"

I pause, taking a deep breath in before answering, "I can feel your hands holding mine, my clothes, and the seat of your car."

The tears have stopped, and so has the crying, so Kayden just coaches me through my breathing.

Eventually, I am able to compose myself, my breathing going back to normal, and tears no longer filling my eyes. Suddenly I was hyper-aware of Kayden still holding my hands.

"Thank you," I say quietly as I pull my hands out of his.

"Of course. Are you feeling better now?"

Nodding, I ask, "I'm fine, but can we keep driving?"

Kayden hesitates for a moment before agreeing, turning the car back on, and pulling back onto the road.

Thank God he didn't ask me what happened.

Neither of us says anything as the ride continues. This time I was the first one to break the silence, "Sorry, I know it's rude to not tell you what happened, I just needed to process. Sorry, I made you stop the car too." I sigh, "I was just thinking about how I'll never see my mom again. And sort of just where she is now."

Kayden stays silent, but I can see him considering his words, "First off, don't apologize. It's okay. I would be more worried if you were completely fine. However, on the topic of the afterlife, I have an answer for you. If you want that answer when your mental state is better, then just ask."

I don't know how to answer him, but thankfully he keeps speaking, "I know you're worried about the future of you and your sisters, but I will tell you that you three will be okay. I can promise you that. You may not believe in him, but I know that the Lord will provide a way."

"Being scared of the future is normal, especially when you've just been given life-changing news, and this isn't to invalidate your worries, but I want you to know that even through the ups and downs in life, God will be there."

Kayden glances at me to make sure I'm listening before saying, "Even if you don't think that God is there for you, or that he's real, you've got Kehlani, Theo, Ashton, and I in your corner."

I don't understand how anyone could be so confident and sure of a god who seemed to be absent all the time. *How and why would his "god," if he was real, want to provide for someone who denies his existence?*

"Thank you for helping me even if I haven't made you want to help me. I can't express how grateful I am for your help. I don't get your Christianity nonsense, but it did make me feel better."

Kayden seems to be contemplating saying something, and it seems like he decides to, "I was in a similar boat as you, and it's not me who can change your heart. I can answer any questions you have, but I can't tell you what to believe."

He what? Who died? I wait for him to continue, but when he doesn't I just nod.

Suddenly a thought occurs to me. "How did you know what coffee to get me? It was what I normally would order."

He grins and says, "I was going to get everyone coffee before and asked for everyone's coffee orders. Kehlani gave me yours. I didn't end up ordering coffee since, as your best friend so kindly reminded me, most people don't drink coffee at five p.m."

I'm genuinely surprised he remembered, but then again he went to med school, so I would hope he has a good memory. We then fall into a rhythm of conversation. The dynamic changes between us, and to be honest... I don't hate it.

Chapter 9

$\mathcal{A}$s soon as we're in the neighborhood of my sister's friend, the mood shifts, and we both fall into silence. I text the twins when we arrive. Kayden stays in the car, and when I get out, Charlie comes running out of the house and jumps into my arms.

Ellie follows out holding a bag, and my heart absolutely shatters when I see her. It looks like she has had every bit of life drained from her.

Quickly, I thank their friend's mother for letting them stay over for a couple of hours. She gives me the normal 'Let me know if you need anything speech. When we get into the car, it's just silent and somber. I give Kayden the address to the house, and he starts driving.

The second we get home, Elianna runs out of the car, and into the house. Charlotte slowly follows Ellie into the house.

I sigh and look at Kayden who just pats my shoulder sympathetically. "They'll be okay. They just need their big sister and a little comfort."

I nod, pushing my emotions back, "You can stay in the guest bedroom if you'd like. I don't want you to go find somewhere to stay since it's already late."

Kayden smiles, "Thank you. I'll take you up on that,

59

but before I go in, I'll get you guys food first. Anything you guys would like?" He asks.

I still don't get why he keeps wanting to help me, or why he even cares so much, but I appreciate it. "If you don't mind getting us food, that would be amazing. The girls' favorite restaurant is La Dolce Vita. I can text you their orders when you get there." I then grab my wallet and give him some money to buy the food.

"Okay, yeah. I'll go get the food. I hope you get through to your sisters. I'll be back soon."

When I walk into the house I'm bombarded by Charlotte who apparently was watching me through the window.

"Adria...Who was that? That definitely wasn't an Uber driver. You know him, who is that, and why did he drive you three hours to come back home?" Charlotte questions the minute I walk in through the door.

"Am I allowed to walk through the door, and take my shoes off before I'm subjected to your interrogation of my life?" I laugh as I ask my sister.

Nodding, she then waits for me as I put my things down. As soon as I'm done, she drags me to the couch, asking me the questions again.

Laughing, I decide to answer, "Okay, okay. That is Kayden. I already know you're going to ask me if he's my boyfriend, no he's not. We're not even friends."

Her eyebrows rise, "Uh huh. Because someone who's not your friend would drive you three hours to see your sisters after your mother passes away."

"Fine, maybe we're friends." I relent, "He's only here because we were about to hang out with Kehlani when I got the call."

"So then why didn't Kehlani or Theo take you?"

"Kehlani and Theo went to the fair before we hung out, and they never got back. Speaking of which, I should

60

probably make sure they're okay." I then grab my phone and ask Kehlani if they had gotten back to the house.

Charlie and I stay silent for a while before the tears start to well up in her eyes. "Ria, what's going to happen to us."

"I'm sorry, I don't know. What I do know is that we will make it work. I'll go speak to Mom's lawyers tomorrow. It's going to be okay." I try reassuring her while giving her a hug.

The tears finally start to flow, "We're really never going to see mom again. We've already lost Dad, now Mom too?"

My heart breaks when Charlotte sobs as she clings to me. I don't know what else to do as I watch my sister break down. *How am I supposed to help her?*

Eventually, her sobs die down. "Where's Ellie?" I say when I realize I haven't seen my other sister since we got out of the car.

"She probably went to our room." Charlie pauses, her face falling. "Ellie…" She takes a deep breath, "Ellie was the one who found Mom on the floor of the kitchen. She took it the hardest."

Oh boy. "Hey, when Kayden gets back, open the door for him. I'm going to go check on Elianna. Will you be okay here by yourself?"

When Charlotte confirms that she would be fine, and will open the door, I bolt upstairs, to attempt to talk to my sister.

Knock. Knock. Knock. "Hey, Ellie. Can I come in? Please?"

The door locks and Ellie yells, "No! Leave me alone! Go hang out with Charlie and that pretty boy I'm pretty sure you're dating that drove us."

"Ellie, come out please, I want to make sure you're okay. There's dinner coming soon. It's your favorite La

61

Dolce Vita." I try.

"Adria! Just leave me alone. I'm not leaving my room, and I'm not hungry. Just go away. I'm sorry that you and Charlotte are so easily able to ignore the fact that Mom died. Well, I was the one who found Mom. So, leave. Me. Alone." I can hear the anger in Ellie's voice, so I decide to give up and head back downstairs.

When I get downstairs, I realize that Kayden has made it back with the food.

"God's blessing? I've never thought of it that way, but I guess in a way you're right. The universe did give me a built-in best friend." Charlie says.

Kayden starts to respond but quiets down when I walk into the living room. "She won't come out. I've tried everything, and she's just stopped answering me too. Has she just been like this since the officers came here earlier?" I cry when I sit down next to my sister. She immediately envelopes me in a hug.

Kayden speaks up tentatively, "I don't want to intrude, but maybe just give her some time to think. We all have different methods of coping, and Elianna's might just be that she wants to stay by herself to think. You can always check on her later, to make sure that she eats something."

"Can we eat now?" Charlie pipes to ask.

Kayden nods for me, and Charlie immediately runs to the kitchen, leaving me alone with him.

He grabs my hand as I start walking to the kitchen. "You can say no, but do you want me to try talking to your sister?" *Ugh. Why is he so sweet?*

"That would be amazing. You don't understand how grateful I am for everything you've done for me and my family. If you can't get her to come out and eat, then that's alright." I say.

"Of course. Are you allowed to bring food upstairs?" When I nod, Kayden runs to the kitchen, and grabs what I

62

assume was the pasta that was meant for Ellie, then runs upstairs.

I follow after a couple of seconds and join Charlie. As I'm opening the pasta dish, and getting a fork I hear Elianna yell, "Adria! Go. Away! How many times do I have to say I'm not coming out of my room!"

Worried, I run upstairs, but before I can make myself known, Kayden says softly, "Hey Elianna. I hope you don't mind me using your full name. I know you're not exactly in a good mental space right now, but both of your sisters want to hang out with you. I brought you food from your favorite restaurant."

"I don't want to eat or go out right now." Ellie sounds closer to the door this time.

"Well if you don't want to go downstairs, you could eat right now. I brought your favorite chicken alfredo. Adria said you could eat upstairs." Kayden says.

The door creaks open, and Ellie sticks her head out. "Okay."

As he hands her the food, he asks, "Can I come in? I want to talk to you." By some miracle, she agrees and lets him in. *Dang, he's good.* I then head back down to the kitchen.

After fifteen minutes Kayden comes back down to the kitchen, but to my surprise, Elianna follows him. I have no idea how he did it, but I'm glad he was able to do it. We spend the rest of the night talking and eating.

My eyes slowly open, as I'm waking up. "Nice outfit Charlie, and I like the blush. Matches your skin color. Now where do you two want to go while your sister deals with the legal stuff?" *Kayden?*

"Thank you? I mean this in the most respectful way

possible, but are you gay?" I need to clap my hand over my mouth after hearing that.

Kayden laughs, "Nope. I am not, I just have a nineteen-year-old sister, and I was the one who had to take her shopping when she started getting into makeup. Kehlani is also one of Theo's best friends, so you know, I usually have to tag along."

I decide that it is time for me to make an appearance. When I get out of my room, both Charlie and Kayden are still laughing, "Why are you two laughing?" Ellie asks. *Guess she had the same idea as me.*

Charlotte slightly blushes, and answers, "I thought he was gay because he mentioned my makeup."

At that answer, Elianna cracks a small smile, before it drops again, and she asks, "So where are we going?"

Kayden shrugs and says, "Wherever you two would like to go. I'm just the driver, and the credit card."

Both my sisters look at each other before saying at the same time, "The mall!"

I laugh at their twin telepathy, and all three of them turn towards me. "Where are you three going? And why?"

Kayden looks at me sheepishly, "Well I was going to ask you, but I figured you needed sleep, so I was going to take your sisters off your hand since you'll be figuring things out with the lawyer later."

"Please can we go, Ria? Please?" Both my sisters give me their best pleading looks. I only last about ten seconds until I give in.

"Fine, but Kayden is not paying for your things. You two are. Promise?" The girls nod their heads, and Kayden tells them to head to the car.

"I'm sorry I didn't tell you. I hope you're not angry." Kayden apologizes.

I smile. *He is too nice.* "It's okay. I don't mind. That would actually be amazing, but I don't know how I would've

64

done this without you." *Well, being nice is new.*

When Kayden leaves with the girls, I get ready. Sighing, I call the lawyer to discuss my mother's will.

"Adria, we're back!" Charlie says at my door when they get home. Sighing, I get up, and check to see the damage they made. *It's been a tough couple of days, they deserve it.*

I leave my room and walk downstairs to join everyone. "I can see you guys are back. And with an unimaginable amount of bags." I raise my eyebrows in suspicion, "Where did you two get the money for all of that?"

Ellie speaks first, "We…uh…Kayden bought some of it for us?"

Before I can start scolding them, Kayden cuts in, "Hold on, don't start losing it yet. I told them I would get those things for them. They never asked. In fact, both of them fought me trying to tell me that I didn't need to buy any of that stuff for them."

Sighing, I say, "Fine, both of you go put your stuff away. After that, I need to talk to you both in my room, and no it's not about the mall."

When they run upstairs I continue, "And Kayden, just because I'm changing the subject, and am going upstairs to tell them what happened doesn't mean you're off the hook. Feel free to do whatever until we're back. It'll take like ten minutes."

Kayden grins and nods before we both head upstairs to our respective rooms.

I really don't want to have this conversation with them.

"Adria, why did you need to talk to us?" Charlie asks when they both walk into the room.

"We need to talk about where you two are going

65

to live, and what's going to happen to the house." Their demeanor immediately changes, "I know you aren't going to like this, but you two aren't going to be living with me. I wasn't listed as your legal guardian in Mom's will."

"Wait, why? That's not fair."

"Where are we going then?"

"Why can't we stay with you?"

Pulling both of them into a hug, I say, "Well to answer all those questions, you're going to live with Avó and Vovô. Look I know you would rather live with me, but I can't take care of you two. Kehlani and I don't have another room, and no one would be able to stay with you the majority of the time. Look, Avó and Vovô are going to live here with you guys until the end of the school year, and from there, we'll decide whether they want to move to Roseburrough, or if you guys will move with them to Greenwood."

When both girls are still silent after a couple of minutes I say, "I know it's a lot to process right now, so just take the rest of the day to think about it. If you guys want to go out with your friends that's cool, or if you want to hide out in your room all day then that's up to you."

Both of them just numbly nod and walk to their rooms. Sighing for what must be the millionth time today, I knock on the guest bedroom door.

"Come in, sweetheart," Kayden says.

I walk in, and he's just sitting up on the bed texting someone, "Again, can you stop calling me sweetheart?"

"I could, but isn't it more fun this way? The irony is the best part. You're feisty, and not-so-sweet, and you don't like me." He grins, and I just roll my eyes, "So what brings you to this room willingly?"

"To interrogate you for spoiling my sisters, and leaving the money I gave you for food yesterday in my room. No idea when you did it, but imagine my surprise. Why are you doing all this? You don't know my sisters at all, and

66

again we're not close. Why are you giving so much?"

His demeanor changes to serious, "Because what you're going through is rough, and draining. It's one of the hardest things a person can go through, especially when you have to take care of your sisters too. I'm just doing whatever I can to lessen the burden for you. Speaking of your sisters, what's going to happen to them?"

I sigh at the change of subject, but I don't have the energy to change it back, "They're going to stay here with my grandparents, who will be moving here until at least the end of the year. The girls did not take it well when I told them they weren't going to live with Kehlani and me. At least they didn't lose it on me. I thought Ellie was going to throw a fit."

Kayden shrugs and says, "I think they're both just so emotionally exhausted, they can't even find it in them to fight anything anymore."

"I guess so. I just desperately hope they will be okay tomorrow." He hums in agreement. "I'm going to go check up on them now. I think I'm going to go to bed after. You can do whatever. Make some food, go out, or something. I'm sorry you got sucked into all this. We can go home tomorrow after my grandparents arrive." I say, the exhaustion just hitting.

"Hey Adria," I turn around as I'm walking towards the door, "God gives you trials that you, yourself *cannot* handle, because when in times of trouble, it is of human instinct to turn to God. Adria, I know God is looking for you. He's looking for that way into your heart, but you just have to let him in. Please let him in, he will make this burden light." I weakly smile and he continues, "Sorry, I know that's not what you want to hear, but I'll be praying for you. Goodnight, Adria."

"Goodnight, Kayden."

Chapter 10

"Elianna! Hurry Up! I have to go!" I yell to my sister, as Charlotte, Avó, Vovô, Kayden, and I stand by the door, ready to leave.

"Okay! I'm coming. I just want to finish eating the food *Kayden* cooked." Ellie yells back. I roll my eyes. All morning she's been telling me how I should bring Kayden all the time just to cook for her. Apparently, my cooking is, and I quote, 'So bland and mediocre that it could kill someone'. *Guess I didn't get the Brazilian genes.*

In the meantime I hug Charlotte, telling her, "Call me anytime you need to. I'll do my best to answer, and I'll always get back to you. I'll try and visit as often as possible." Charlie hugs me back, and we both start crying again.

When we break apart, I give my grandparents a hug thanking them for moving in to take care of my sisters. My grandmother pulls me close and whispers, "I know you're being strong for your sisters, but you need to let yourself grieve too. Take care of yourself, Neta."

"Okay. Okay. I'm done eating. Why is everyone crying?" Ellie interrupts, running to the door.

Charlie answers for me, "Because Ria and Kayden are leaving. So say goodbye."

Ellie's face drops and she quickly gives me a hug.

She's shutting down again. Ouch. But I can't blame her though.

We start to head over to the car, Elianna staying back by the front door.

"I'm going to use the bathroom before we leave," Kayden says. Nodding, I continue hugging my family and saying goodbye.

"Bring him back sometime, Ria. I like him." Charlie says, as both my grandparents agree with her.

"He's kind and good, Neta. Keep him around." Avó says, smiling.

Shaking my head, I say, "Sure. No promises though. I am grateful for what he's done this weekend, but if he will stay around? I don't know"

Wondering where he is, I look around only to see that he's talking to my sister. She's deep in thought, as he's explaining something. *I will never understand him, but he's getting through to her.* Elianna looks up and continues talking to him, cracking a small smile. *Why couldn't I get through to her though? What did he say to her?*

They both walk over once they're finished talking. To my surprise, Ellie says bye to me, hugging me and telling me to stay safe. Both my sisters hug Kayden and say thank you for everything he's done. My heart warms at the brighter smiles both my sisters have while talking to him.

We get in the car, and take off for the three-hour drive. "Kayden..." I say tentatively, "What did you say to Ellie that convinced her to come say bye? And to put a smile on her face?"

"Not much. I told her my situation with Samuel."

I cut in, "Who's that?"

Kayden gives me a sad smile, "He is my younger brother. He passed away due to a heart defect he was born with. Sam's the reason I wanted to be a surgeon. Specifically a trauma surgeon."

I smile, "That's sweet. I'm sorry for your loss."

I see him nod lightly, "Brooklyn took his death the hardest. I was always hanging out with Theo, but she and Sam stuck together like glue. It took us almost a year to get her to talk. But continuing my story, I told her that Brooklyn went through a similar thing with Sam. I also gave her some Bible verses that helped us both get through his death."

I open my mouth to protest, and he stops me, "Look, I didn't tell her anything about having to believe the verses. I just told her that they helped my family get through that rough patch in our lives. I didn't tell her much more."

"Okay. I guess she's old enough to know what's real and what's not. Thank you for talking to her. It means so much to me. I don't know how you got through to her so easily, but I'm glad you did."

The whole way home, there is no awkward tension, which genuinely surprises me. Kayden and I talk to each other the whole way home about everything. Work, family, friends, a lot of things. I am pleasantly surprised. *Maybe I judged him too quickly...*

> *Me: What time will you be here?*
>
> *Damien: When I get there. I'm kidding. I'll be there in fifteen minutes.*
>
> > *Me: Okay. Kehlani will have left by then. Bring snacks. I need food.*

"Adria, I'm leaving to go to a school thing!" Kehlani yells as I'm telling Damien that she's leaving.

I walk out of my room and stand by the door. "Great, have fun with the middle school children, and their parents tonight! I'll be home for the rest of the night unless we go

71

out to dinner. Damien's coming over for a movie night. You can join us after your school event if you want."

"Yeah, I might. Depends on when I'm done. My ringer's on, so if you need me, just text." Kehlani's face falls, and I know she still feels guilty for not being there when I needed to go to Roseburrough.

"Kehlani… It's okay. You and Theo were in the desert. It's not like you could've controlled whether or not your car broke down. Plus that idiot forgot his phone at home, and you had no internet. It's fine. I'm fine. The twins are fine. And Kayden still drove me. That was extremely awkward by the way." I say to reassure her.

Kehlani hums in amusement, "Oh yeah, how could I forget? It must've been terrible hanging out with a six-foot, green-eyed, brown-haired guy all weekend." I gave her a look, and she sighs and says, "Fine. Fine. I know that means nothing. But seriously, how was it awkward? You said he was good at helping with your sisters, and you."

I make a face, "Yeah, it's borderline weird. He's one of the nicest and sweetest guys I've ever met. I feel like there has to be a catch. He was my saving grace when it came to Ellie. I still don't know how I would've dealt with her if he wasn't there."

I can tell Kehlani's confused now, "So you two are friends now? I still can't tell if you're trying to stay away from him."

"Can you really still hate a guy after he drove you six hours round trip to go see your sisters after your mother passed away? Then stays for two days while helping both you and your sisters as you're all grieving and having mental breakdowns? He did all that out of the freaking goodness of his heart, and he barely knows me. How am I supposed to dislike him, even though he keeps bringing up the Bible and crap?" I sigh, thinking of Mom again.

Kehlani just nods, "Okay, I don't know what to say

to that. I do need to go, so I'll see you after work. Bye!" With that, she bounds out of the house.

I go to my room to grab some blankets and put them on the couch. As I'm getting drinks, the doorbell rings.

"Julie." Damien drags out the nickname, I'm sorry. I'm so sorry I didn't see your message, and didn't get to take you to Roseburrough."

"It's fine. You were working. The twins missed seeing you though."

He nods, "So, how's it going?"

I snort, "Rough. It's just hitting me that both my parents are gone."

"Don't worry, you'll see her again in another life." He gives me a hug, "On that note, how are the baby Sousas?"

I shake my head, "Not good. Well, Ellie's not handling it well, though it was better before I left. Charlie, I think, is more worried about Ellie than to be grieving. We'll see where that leads us though." The somberness of the conversation dulls the energy, "Okay let's be done being depressing. Movie time?"

We start the movie, but around a half hour in, I get a text.

> ***Kayden****: Hey, Adria. Is there any way you could give Elianna Brooklyn's phone number? When we talked before we left, I told her that I would have Brooklyn reach out. I thought that Brooklyn could help her since she went through a similar thing with Samuel's passing.*

> > ***Me****: Yeah. I don't mind. Is Brooke okay with giving Ellie her phone number?*

Kayden: Yeah. I told Brooke
about Ellie, and she wanted to
speak to her especially to help
her. I think Ellie reminds her a bit
of herself.

Me: Sounds awesome. I'll send
Brooke Ellie's number.

Kayden: Awesome. How are you
doing?

"Family?" Damien asks. I shake my head, "Wait, I
thought that Kehlani was at a school thing.

"Excuse me? Do you think I don't have any other
friends other than you and Kehlani? What if I was talking to
another friend?" I say insulted.

Damien gives me a look, "Oh really?"

"Fine. You're not wrong." I relent. "It was Kayden
though. He wanted to send Ellie Brooklyn's phone number.
Apparently she could help with Ellie."

"Oh okay. How nice of him." Damien then turns
back to watch the movie.

Me: Meh. Could be better. Better
than yesterday, but still not great.
I think it hasn't hit me just yet.

Kayden: I'm sorry. If you need
anything, especially prayer, and
yes I do realize that you don't
believe in that, just let me know.

Me: Kayden, I know you mean
well, but I don't want any of that.
Get the hint that I don't care about
your religion. Thank you for the
offer, but I'm good. Have a good
rest of your day.

__Kayden__: Alright. I'm sorry I
overstepped. Have a good day.
> *__Me__: It's fine. Thank you for*
> *checking in, and for everything*
> *you've done for us over the*
> *weekend.*

After the movie has finished, Damien and I get some food from a nearby restaurant. We spent the rest of the night talking and hanging out. Kehlani never ended up hanging out with us. I think she went to hang out with Theo after.

Chapter 11

The next couple of weeks are difficult. There were days when I couldn't even bring myself to get out of bed, much less go to work. It took me a while, some ups and downs, but eventually, with some help, I learn to live with the grief. I took three days off of work to make sure I was mentally stable before heading back. Eventually, though, I do have to go back, and I pour myself into work.

Six more hours. Just six more hours. The radio crackles and my instant reaction is to groan, "Dispatch to two-seventeen."

I sigh, and pick up the radio, answering, "Two-seventeen to dispatch, what's the situation?"

"We've got a demonstration on Blackthorn Avenue, near the mall. The reason for the demonstration is still unknown. The caller reported a heated discussion between four different individuals there. It doesn't seem like it will get violent, but it's been requested that we check it out first." The dispatcher reports.

"Alright. I'll head over there right now. My ETA is ten minutes. Have back-up on standby as a precaution." I respond.

"Copy."

As I pull up to Blackthorn Street, my gut tells me something's going to happen, but I push it away and report to dispatch that I've arrived. I then get out of the car only to hear a man screaming at another while two women stand by him. "YOU ARE IGNORANT AND INTOLLERANT! HOW—" *Oh boy. This is off to a great start.*

I interrupt, "Hey, I'm Officer Sousa from the Silver Valley Police Department. What seems to be the problem here?"

One of the two women present speaks up first, "Nothing Officer, we were just having a disagreement. We will be on our way, right Madison?"

She looks at her friend, and the other girl, who I assume is Madison, says, "We didn't mean to cause a disturbance."

I nod at them both, "Go ahead, I won't hold you up." They hurriedly run away. As they're running away, I turn to the two men still angrily arguing. Well, one is angrily yelling, and the other amusedly answering back. "And what's the reason that you both are causing a public disturbance?"

The man who was previously yelling turns to me, his voice harsh, "Nothing. We weren't doing anything. You can go back to doing your job if you can call it that."

His words catch me by surprise, "Excuse me, sir?"

Before he can speak again, the other man cuts in, "I apologize for him, ma'am. Our disagreement was on the need for a demonstration against police brutality. I was simply explaining that it's a rare thing, especially more recently. The discussion got out of hand, and for my part in it, I apologize."

I let him go, and as he is leaving, he says, "Thank you for your service, ma'am. It's much appreciated by many." I don't say anything, but it felt good to hear that the job I was doing wasn't going completely unnoticed.

I turn back to the man, and instead of leaving, he says, "Leave us alone. Go back to "helping" other people. You don't deserve to be paid for by our taxes."

I want to argue, but it would be pointless, "I'm sorry that you feel that way, but you are causing a public disturbance, and if you are going to protest, please do not get in others' faces to prove your point."

My words do not amuse him, and before leaving, he spits in my face saying, "Look at everyone here to protest the funding of the police. We will find a way to cut your funding."

Annoyed and tired, I head back to my car once he leaves. I drive down a couple of blocks before picking up my radio to report what had happened, "Two-seventeen to dispatch."

"Copy"

"It was nothing. They were having a demonstration, and one person just did not agree with the demonstration. Once I arrived, the discussion was resolved."

"Understood. Stay where you are or in that area in case the protest escalates. We have two other units also in the area since a physical altercation seems possible here."

I nod out of habit, but when I realize the dispatcher couldn't see me, I say, "Copy."

Three more hours. Three more hours. I'm exhausted and am counting down the hours until I can get off of work.

BANG! BANG! BANG!

Frick. Frick. Frick. That sounded like it was coming from the mall.

I turn the car on and start driving towards the mall. As I'm driving, I pick up the radio and report frantically,

79

"I think we have a 10-71 in progress. Shots fired. People running, tell the other units to head back towards Blackthorn Mall"

The radio crackles, as I'm parking, "Copy."

"Three-twenty heading over to the Blackthorn Mall. ETA is three to seven minutes." A muffled male voice says

Another male voice chimes in, "Seven-thirty-two headed over to Blackthorn Ave. ETA is five to ten minutes."

"One-sixty-eight heading over to the Blackthorn Mall. ETA is five to ten minutes." The last voice reports."

I'm grabbing a rifle as I say, "Copy"

BANG! BANG! BANG!

I'm cursing under my breath as I hear people screaming. *This isn't going to end well.*

When I get out, I start running towards the shots, only stopping to help guide some people to the nearest open building. The shots just keep coming and coming. I will my legs to run faster. *I need to get to the shooter before someone gets hurt.*

There is a pause in the ringing out of shots, and I slow down, trying to be cautious of the shooter. I'm walking towards where I had heard the shots, trying to catch my breath as the first of my three backups arrive.

"Where are the shots coming from?" He asks.

My hands are still stuck to my rifle aiming towards where I'd heard the shots, "My two o'clock. Let's move."

He nods and then we both start jogging towards my two o'clock, waiting for the shots to restart. About five seconds later the shots ring out again, and we bolt towards the sound.

When we get there, we spot a skinny young man shooting towards the library from the end of the parking lot.

I'm panting as I report, "Black shirt. Young male." I'm breathing heavily, "Dark blue jeans. Brown hair." I pause for a moment trying to identify the weapon, "Holding a Glock. Two officers are on the scene. Chasing down from the east side of the Library. Send units to the west. Injuries present, and death likely."

Once I finish reporting, I look at the second officer and say, "Get behind the black car now." He nods at my instruction.

I run further down the parking lot than he does and hide behind a red car. Holding up the Colt M4 Carbine, I start to aim towards the shooter. The second officer follows, aiming his Glock 48

My heart rate is rising quickly, adrenaline pumping in my blood. *Breathe. Calm down and focus.* I give the signal, and we both step slightly out of the protection of the car and start shooting.

BANG! BANG! BANG!

The radios are still on so I report when there's a break in shots, "I've got a hit! Leg hit I believe!"

My voice booms as I yell at the shooter, "Stay where you are! PUT THE WEAPON DOWN!"

BANG! BANG!

The supporting officer yells, "DROP THE GUN!" It's clear the shooter is not listening to our demands.

BANG! BANG! BANG!

I'm cursing again. *Crap. He won't stop. He's still shooting, and now it's right at us.*

Careful to stay somewhat protected by the car, I peek out the side of the car carefully. Taking a deep breath, I aim quickly, and fire.

BANG! BANG! BANG!

I hold my breath, and we watch the shooter collapse on the floor. I let out a sigh of relief.

"STAY WHERE YOU ARE! STAY WHERE YOU ARE! DON'T MOVE! DROP THE WEAPON." I bellow while I walk towards him, my rifle still up, ready to shoot at the first sign of danger. Movement from one o'clock catches my eye as we walk closer. Two officers step out from behind the pillar also holding firearms.

When we're close enough to the shooter, I kick the dropped gun to the side, and my partner steps in to grab him.

The third officer speaks into the radio, "We're going to need multiple EMTs stat. What's their ETA? We have several injured, and some that may be dead. We've yet to check the perimeters."

As my partner is handcuffing the shooter, I instruct him to watch the man and wait for the paramedics who would have to take him to the Silver Valley St. Paul's hospital.

To one of the officers that came from the west, "You. Officer Figueroa?" He nods so I continue, "Take half of the officers that are arriving to check the perimeters and the amount of fatalities and injuries. You will take the west, and I'll take the east along with the inside of the library."

He nods, confirming, "Understood ma'am."

I turn to the officers who have just arrived and say, "Half of you! I need you to go check the westside for those injured and hiding throughout the area including the library." Half the officers start running, "The other half! You're under Officer Figueroa. You will receive your instructions from him."

I decided to start in the library first, "Silver Valley Police Officer! To anyone who is currently inside this building, the threat has been neutralized! Stay where you are until the paramedics arrive!"

As I'm walking through the shattered library doors, the sight I'm met with makes my heart drop to my stomach. *Blood everywhere.*

A man and a woman lay on the floor seemingly dead at the entrance. I check both of their pulses. *Nothing.* The further I walk into the library, the worse it gets. Another man lays dead seeming to have bled out as well. I check his pulse, and again nothing.

A cry catches my attention, so I run towards it. A young man, probably still in his late teens, was grazed by a bullet and had blood gushing down the side of his leg.

Taking a deep breath, I ask, "Did the bullet go straight through your leg or just graze it?"

The teenager fists the edge of his shirt as he grits out, "I think it went all the way through when it hit my leg." He pauses, hissing in pain, "Is there anything you can do to stop the bleeding?"

I nod and quickly check his leg to confirm no artery was hit and that the bullet had gone all the way through. When it's confirmed, I get up and start running towards the front seat to get a first aid kit. As soon as I find the kit and a couple of pillows, I run straight back towards the young man. "This is going to hurt, but until the paramedics get here, you're going to need it."

The brown-haired teenager nods, giving me his approval. I grab the tourniquet, laying the stick on his calf, and pulling tightly in the self-adhering band. "This is where it's going to hurt, so hold onto the pillows I found.

I start twisting the windlass, and he instantly grabs the pillow to yell into. As I keep twisting he starts gritting his teeth. It is obvious that the pain is almost too much.

"Okay, one more twist, and... I'm done!" I check my watch before writing the time on the tourniquet. "The bleeding has stopped, but you can't keep your leg in the tourniquet for long. An EMT will be here soon. Don't move."

"Yes, ma'am." He agrees.

Checking to make sure he was okay before I leave? I then get up and speak into the radio, "What are the EMTs' ETA?"

"Two ambulances have already arrived."

Thankfulness washes over me, "send several of them inside the library. There are three dead inside, and a teenager by the bathrooms whose leg was shot. He seems to be doing fine. I've applied a tourniquet for the time being."

"Copy" The officer responds.

"I'm going to check the rest of the library. Let me know once you've found him."

"Copy."

I continue to walk through the library, stopping to tell several people who were hiding that it was clear to go outside. I warn them that they may be stopped by an officer to be checked or to give a witness account.

Once every area in the library is cleared, I meet with several more units of officers who have completed their checks and are taking notes for the report. Some EMTs are speaking to those who are only shaken up, some who are caring for the injured, and then some EMTs who are rushing others to the hospital.

I let out a breath I didn't know I was holding. *It's over. We've got a long road ahead, but the shooting is over.*

Chapter 12

$\mathcal{L}$ooking at the clock, it hits me that it's already eight. The adrenaline is slowly starting to wear off from my body. *I'm exhausted.* Quickly checking that my notes and weapons are all in the car with me, I start the car. And with that, I start driving over to the hospital to write down the reports on the shooter, those who have died, and those who have been injured.

It's just a couple of notes. You can do this. Everything's going to be okay.

When I walk into the hospital, I head straight towards the front desk, "Good evening, I'm Officer Adria Sousa from the Silver Valley police department." I pause to show her my badge before continuing, "Is there any way I can speak to a nurse or doctor to discuss the casualties and injuries from the shooting?"

The receptionist answers, "Yes, of course, Officer. Unfortunately, many of our doctors are busy due to the shooting, so I will tell one of them to be out as soon as they're available. In the meantime, you can sit over there by the couch."

Nodding, I go to sit down for the first time in hours. The adrenaline has officially worn off, and my body slumps in the chair. As I'm sitting there in silence, my thoughts start to overwhelm my brain. *How many were hurt? How many were killed? Was I responsible for any of the killings because of a stray bullet? What happened to the shooter? Is he alive? Who is he? Why did he even start the shooting?*

Before it gets too much, the receptionist comes back out. "Officer Sousa, I've found a doctor who is available to speak to you."

Grateful for the distraction, I get up, ready to get the answers for my report so I can head home. I know it's selfish considering people have just lost their lives, or are fighting for their lives, but I can't feel anything right now.

The doctor who meets with me is extremely kind, and patient. I'm grateful that she doesn't comment on my visible exhaustion, and patiently answers any questions I have on the victims of the shooting.

"Currently we have eight patients in critical condition. I believe six or seven are in surgery right now. It's a miracle that some of them made it here on time, but either way, we are grateful that you were able to stop the shooter in time. Unfortunately, the number found dead on the scene was six. Luckily though, everyone survived the ambulance ride. It is unknown how many patients are currently injured. I will have someone give you a call once we have counted," the doctor explains.

I remember something and ask, "There was a young adult, maybe in his late teens. He showed up with a tourniquet and had been shot in the leg. Do you have any updates on how he is?"

She smiles warmly, and it's slightly unsettling. *How is she smiling right now? I'm so drained it's hard to even speak.* "Yes, I can check on his notes. Just give me a second." I wait for a couple of seconds as she types on her keyboard. "It looks to be here, that he is okay. Nothing too seriously damaged. He will have to stay for a couple of days for observation, but it seems he'll make a full recovery."

I sigh a breath of relief, "Thank you so much for checking, now can we discuss the conditions that the rest of the patients are currently in?"

Around an hour later, I have finished taking all the notes I need from the doctor. I thank her, and head to the lobby to quickly jot down some of the information I have received on my report.

Six dead on scene.

Eight were badly injured.

"Adria? Are you okay? Why are you here?" Someone says, interrupting my concentration.

I know that voice. My head pops up at the familiar deep voice, "Kayden, of course, you're on the clock right now. I'm fine, thank you for asking. Just numb."

"I just got off the clock. I was assisting with surgery on one of the injured. Mind if I take a seat?" He gestures to the chair beside me.

"Go ahead. If I said no, you'd still sit there." I say

"I wouldn't but that's beside the point. What happened? Why are you here?" He asks.

I sigh and say, "You'd never believe it if I told you. I was the one who took care of the Blackthorn Shooting. I'm here taking notes of the victims' conditions."

Kayden's face turns white. "Oh dear. Are you okay? Did you need anything else from the hospital?"

"Like I said, It hasn't hit me yet. I haven't had time to sit down and process what had just happened. I'm still numb."

We're sitting in silence for a while before he asks, "What's going on in that brain of yours?"

I sigh, finishing the note I'm writing before answering, "Nothing. Absolutely nothing. I'm beat from this. The shooting happened at the end of a twelve-hour shift so I'm beat. I'm alright now, just numb. We'll see how that changes in twenty-four hours."

Kayden nods sympathetically, and I continue, "I can't do this. I've just barely lost my mother, and then I had to walk through a library filled with people who died because of a mentally insane person."

He opens his mouth as if to say something but I cut him off, "I'm not telling you this to gain sympathy, I'm telling you this because I just need to talk about it. I'm so tired and mentally drained. I don't even know what to do anymore."

"I am so sorry. I'm not saying this out of sympathy or pity, I say it because I understand what being that mentally exhausted is like. What you had to witness today had to have been grueling."

I sigh, "I'm sorry, I know you had to deal with the people who were shot too. You were in there for some of the surgeries. How are you doing? And just as importantly, how are they doing?"

"Look at you, still thinking of me even though you've just had to deal with something horrifying." I give Kayden a weak smile, "I'm alright. Obviously, it sucks seeing people who'd been injured, but I didn't deal with anyone in critical condition today. The ones that I did have to see, although it may take some time for recovery, I don't think anyone is too seriously injured."

"Yep, it really, really, really messed with me walking into the Blackthorn Library, and having to find the dead bodies." I sigh. "What about the ones in critical condition? Have you received any news on them?"

Kayden's face falls when I ask, "I'm sorry, I don't know. I wasn't dealing with that area tonight."

"Look sorry to cut our "reunion" short, but I've been working since eight or nine this morning, and I'd like to head home. I won't be able to process anything until I'm alone." I say.

He nods, and we both get up, and Kayden decides

88

he's going to walk me to my car. I don't have the energy to argue against it.

"I'll see you. Bye, Kayd." I say as I'm getting in my car.

He starts to walk away, "Goodbye Ria, it was nice to see you." The nickname annoys me, but honestly, I can't find it in me to fight back.

When I get home, I quickly take off my shoes and throw my keys on the counter before retiring to my room. I collapse against the door. For a couple of minutes, I simply sit there, not a thought in my brain, everything feeling numb. But unfortunately, the emptiness doesn't last long.

Oh my gosh. I could've lost my life. The bullets were so close to me. How am I alive? Why am I alive?

The revelation shocks me, but as always one dark thought leads to another.

What if that first shot got him down? The three people who died inside the library might be alive. I just can't hold it together anymore. The dam breaks, and I begin sobbing. I give up. I give up on holding these emotions in. I don't know what to do.

I couldn't even aim well enough to stop him the first time. Six people died because I couldn't get my shot right in time. Eight are critically injured, and many are injured right now. What have I done? Why couldn't I do enough?

I sit there sobbing in a curled-up ball for several minutes, and then my phone buzzes. *I need the distraction.* I take a couple of deep breaths, hoping that they will calm me down. With blurry eyes and shaking hands, I pick up my phone only to see a text message from Kayden.

Kayden: *Hey Adria. I know it's*

late, and I don't even know if
you're awake, but the Lord has
just put it on my heart to share
this verse with you.

"And He said to me, "My grace is
sufficient for you, for My strength
is made perfect in weakness." 2
Corinthians 12:9a.

I know you might just ignore it,
but please, just put some thought
into it. Adria. God is searching
for you. He wants you to know
him and cast every burden you
have upon him.

I also just wanted to check up on
you. I know that everything you've
just gone through cannot be easy
to process.

Why he always has to catch me when I'm having
a mental breakdown, I will never know. And for goodness
sake, can he not talk about his stupid religion for one freaking
second? I'm sobbing again, and I decide not to answer him,
not wanting to deal with any of my emotions.

I quickly grab some clothing and run to the bathroom
to take a shower. I turn the knob in the shower to as hot as
possible, wanting to scrub off every memory of today that I
possibly can. Once I finish, I get ready for bed and climb in
utterly exhausted. I just want to fall asleep and escape this
never-ending nightmare.

But as I'm lying there, my thoughts will not come
to a rest. All I can think about are the lifeless eyes of the

couple I'd seen, the pain in the eyes of the man who had bled out, and the feeling of their cold hands when I checked for their pulse. Vivid pictures of the blood splattered through the library plague my mind.

*Their families will **never** get to say goodbye to their loved ones. And I'm partly to blame for that.*

To make matters worse, after tossing and turning, the phrase '*made perfect in weakness*' will not leave my mind. *Kayden, I despise you for this. All I want is to go to bed, and you just had to send me something that would keep me up.* I know it wasn't his intention, but I can't be bothered to be logical right now. I'm tired of being strong. I'm tired of holding it all in for everyone. I'm tired of pretending I don't have emotions. And for the third time that night, I break down in tears.

God, if you're real? Why is this happening to me? Make it stop, please. Make whatever is making me feel like this stop. Please just numb my pain. I can't take it anymore.

I've hurt so many people and their families. I couldn't protect them like I swore I would. WHAT IS THIS GOD? My friends keep telling me that your grace is sufficient. What grace could you possibly have for me? Where is your grace? How dare you lie to me and say you have grace for me? HOW COULD YOU FORGIVE ME FOR THIS? I killed someone today for goodness' sake.

Right then and there, it hits me.

*Oh my gosh...**I just killed someone.***

Chapter 13

"Adria, where are you?" Kehlani yells into the house when she gets home from work. I'm still in bed, but I don't move. I don't have the energy or the will to get up.

Knock. Knock. I'm not getting the door. *Knock. Knock.* "Adria. Get up. I brought you dinner. Why are you still asleep at six p.m.?" *Is she going to stand there until I get up...*

After a couple of minutes, there's no more knocking, so I turn over in my bed, wanting to go back to sleep. "Adria? Are you okay? I'm going in." *Ugh. Really?* She opens the door, and when she does, "Holy..."

"Kehlani. Go away, I'm not in the mood." I grumble.

I can feel her looking around at the clothes from yesterday tossed on the floor, and me still in bed tangled in my sheets.

"Adria...I mean this with love, but what is wrong with you? Are you okay? What's going on? You're never one to stay in bed like this" When I sit up to look at her, the slight playfulness in her expression goes away.

I look at her, and say sarcastically, "Oh yeah. I'm totally perfect and amazing." Worry crosses Kehlani's face, "Yeah. I'm just great after having to deal with the Blackthorn shooting."

She freezes in shock. "Oh my... Are you okay? How are you doing? Is that why you got home so late?"

I stare at her dead in the eye, annoyed with the stupid question, "How do you think I'm doing? I just watched a person die. Six people died on the scene, three of whom I found dead in the library. Two people died last night due to injuries and because I couldn't get the shooter down fast enough. I couldn't get them to the hospital fast enough. I watched a teenage boy start to bleed out from getting shot. He's alive but he's in pain, and Lord knows what he was planning to do with his life. The injury to his leg could be detrimental. Oh yeah, and I killed someone. So yeah, I'm totally fine.

Kehlani just stands there awkwardly, not knowing what to do. She then decides to run to me and give me a hug. "I'm so sorry that all that happened to you."

I'm frozen as my best friend is hugging me. I feel bad that I'm not moving, but I can't bring myself to move and hug her back. "I...I just...I just don't know how to feel. I don't want to feel anything."

Kehlani sits up on my bed to listen, "Sure I stopped the shooter, whatever, whoop-de-do. He killed eight different people and counting. I didn't get there fast enough. My first shots hit his leg, and they weren't enough to stop him. He kept shooting. I didn't stop him fast enough. My error in aim cost him his life."

Remembering last night breaks me. "I killed him the second time, Kehlani. My aim was off again. I was supposed to hit him in a non-fatal area of the body. He died because my aim was off. There were at least two other people who died from their wounds. I didn't get there in time. If I had, maybe they would still be here. Their families never got to say goodbye. It's my fault that their families will have to see their bodies lifeless and cold"

"Ria...I'm so sorry."

94

I snap, "Kehalni! Sorry isn't going to do anything! They're dead! They're gone!" I want to feel bad, but I can't bring myself to calm down.

"My bad. Wrong choice of words. I mean I'm sorry you're feeling that pain and guilt. You did your best, and you stopped the shooter from potentially hurting more people. I know you missed, but you were being shot at and under fire. You're not in the wrong for ending the shooter's life. You hit his leg first which is what you were supposed to do, and he didn't stop. That was on him." I sigh. I guess she's right, but knowing something, and believing it is a different thing.

"Adria, look at me." I follow her instruction, "Their families aren't going to blame you for their deaths. I'm sure they aren't thrilled, but they know you tried. They know you successfully stopped the shooter." She gives me another hug, and this time, I break down sobbing in her arms.

I'm choking on my words when I say, "Kiki, they're still all gone. At least eight innocent lives were lost. What if the other six lose their lives too? I'd be partially responsible for some of their deaths"

Both Kehlani and I stay silent, not knowing what else to say. Kehlani just holds me as I sobbed my eyes out. I'm not really crying for myself, at least not in the beginning anyway. I am crying for those who just lost their lives, and for their families who would never get to hear their voices again.

Releasing me once my cries die down, Kehlani carefully says, "You might not be ecstatic to hear me suggest this, but I'm going to anyway because it seems like the perfect time. So can I pray for you?"

"I will take anything at this point. I don't believe in Christianity or your god, but I'm desperate so go ahead." It does not escape my memory that I had called out to her god last night before I fell asleep.

Kehlani grabs my hand and starts praying, "Lord, I

95

bring you this child of yours. I know that right now her mind is going wild and running around. The thoughts of guilt I know are there, would you just place your hand over her to calm those thoughts filled with pain and confusion. Would You let her know that your grace and love are enough for her?"

"Would you calm down those warring thoughts and help her understand that by her quick thinking, she saved more people from being hurt. God. Let her know that you're there for her as she's going through what I'm sure is one of the darkest moments of her life. Help her to understand how much you love her." I'm crying again as she's praying.

Her grip on my hands tighten. "God, please give her strength as her flesh and heart are failing. For You said in Psalm seventy-three that during times of weakness, You would be the strength that guides us through. God, would You be the one to give her strength to continue through this valley? Lord, I give this beautiful and strong woman to You, and I pray that even after this prayer she will realize the yearning she has in her heart for You. And in Jesus' name, I pray, Amen." As she closes her prayer, tears are streaming down my face, and my lungs are begging for air.

When did Kehlani start crying? When both of our sobs finally die down, I sit up on my bed, wipe my tears, and say, "Thank you. Thank you for being here with me, and for not trying to explain how I should be feeling. And for reiterating the importance of everything I did. I was so focused on the bad, that I forgot about the brighter side. How you knew some of my thoughts without me telling you, I don't know, but I appreciate the prayer."

"I'm your best friend and roommate. I know what you think. Just remember what I said, God's always got you. In your weakness and in your strength, you just need to ask for it."

I roll my eyes, "My gosh, are you and Kayden in

96

cahoots? Because right before I fell asleep last night he said essentially the same thing. Speaking of which, I don't think I ever responded to him."

"No, he didn't say anything to me. I honestly just found out about the shooting while I was teaching." Something clicks in her brain, "Wait hold on…How did Kayd know what happened? Did you see him yesterday? What did he say?"

"Yeah, I saw him yesterday. He was at the hospital where the victims were being treated. I guess he was taking care of some of the less injured patients that night. We talked for a bit before I got too tired and left."

I turn around to grab my phone, "He said to me, 'Hi Adria. I know it's late, and I don't even know if you're awake, but the Lord has just put it on my heart to share this verse with you.
'And He said to me, 'My grace is sufficient for you, for My strength is made perfect in weakness.' 2 Corinthians 12:9a'

I know you might just ignore it, but please, just put some thought into it. Adria. God is searching for you. He wants you to know him and cast every burden you have upon him'"

When I finish reading, Kehlani starts to tentatively say, "Maybe God's trying to say something to you Ria. He's looking for you, and he knows that right now maybe, just maybe, your heart is softened enough to listen to what He's trying to tell you."

I start saying, "I don't know…" I stop to think, "You, Kayden, Ashton, and Theo have it all figured out. And I've asked all of you how that is. Every time your answer is 'Because of God'. I don't get how a religion could do that, Kiki. Blind faith in what? I just don't see how you do that."

"It's not blind faith, Ria. From our perspective, we're here for one reason only, to be a light in the darkness. Sure, there's going to be times of uncertainty, but God always

97

provides. After all, He provides for the sparrow, so how much more would He provide for us." Kehlani explains, her face lighting up.

It honestly intrigues me how her whole demeanor lights up with excitement when she's talking about God. How do they all have such confidence in their future? Why are they still excited even after the different things that have put them through hell? I don't know, but instead of resenting it like I would normally do, I want it. I'm tired of feeling like I'm constantly stuck in pain and darkness. I want to be able to live my life with joy and confidence in my future.

Kehlani looks at me, seemingly worried, "I know you're going to hate this idea, but please just hear me out. I think it would be beneficial, and answer all the questions you have. Would you go to church with me on Wednesday?"

I open my mouth to say no, but something in me hesitates. *Is it bad I'm considering it? I don't know. I still don't believe it, but I want what they have. I want to know why they have this joy and light about them.*

I take a deep breath, "You know what, maybe. We'll see how I feel in two days. But as of right now, sure."

Kehlani froze in surprise, "You'll actually go with me to church?" I want to laugh at how surprised she is.

"Yeah. I think so."

Kehlani smiles, and texts someone. "Okay now, I brought some food, and it's getting cold, so let's go eat."

"Okay. Just let me respond to Kayden since I kind of ghosted him yesterday." I say as she walks out of the room.

Me: Hey, I'm doing okay. I don't know how to explain it, nor do I have the energy for it right now, but I'm doing better than when you saw me yesterday. Thank you for checking up on me.

"Adria! Food!" Kehlani yells.

I laugh, "Okay I'm coming. No need to lose your mind."

Chapter 14

On Monday, February 13, 2040, a Silver Valley Police Officer was involved in an officer-involved shooting in the area of the Blackthorn Mall and the Silver Valley Library...

I cannot tear my eyes away from the public release report. I know that if my name gets out to the public, I will be attacked for killing the shooter. Sighing, I start to finish writing the report. Soon, I receive his lab reports on the weapons, his DNA, etc...

Name: Christian Jasper Galloway

Age: Thirty-two

Race: White

Motivation: Unknown yet. Seemed to be mentally unstable. Assumed to be an argument held with another individual.

Notes: Weapon: Glock 48

Casualties: Eight dead, six in critical condition, and seven injured.

Well, this was unhelpful. I place the basic information into both the public statement and the report that I will have to turn in.

My memory is honestly extremely hazy of that night after the shooter went down, so I went to grab the body camera footage. As I'm heading back from grabbing the USB, Chief Kaiser stops me, "Officer Sousa. How is the investigation going?"

"It's going well. As of right now, it seems as though the shooter acted alone. It also seemed like he wasn't in his right mind. We're doing a further investigation, but as of right now, it looks as though he acted on account of a disagreement with another. I have also nearly finished the press report. It should be done by tomorrow." I report.

Chief Kaiser shakes his head, "Such a tragedy that his mental state was unknown until many were hurt. I'm glad your investigation is going well. I trust that you and the other officers involved in the matter will finalize both the investigation and the reports. I would like you to be cautious for several weeks though. If your name gets out, there's a large chance that you will face backlash."

"Thank you, sir. I will be cautious. I hate that this is what we have to do because the narrative is skewed, but it's not like we can argue."

Chief Kaiser then says, "Completely off the record, and I'm not asking you as your boss, but as a fellow police officer. How are you doing mentally?"

I fidget with my fingers for a bit before responding, "I'm doing okay sir. It's obviously not the easiest, but I'm doing alright."

"Adria, as well as you're hiding it, I was once in your position." He smiles warmly, "I can tell it has taken a toll on you. If you need someone to talk to, I am here, but if I do suggest you talk to someone about it whether it be a friend or family."

Unsurprisingly, he can tell that I am stretching the truth, "Yeah, I've spoken to Kehlani about the guilt and it helped quite a bit."

"Ah okay. Well, I will let you go then, but keep in mind that seeing a therapist might be good for you. It's

102

normal for officers to go into therapy after a difficult call."

I nod, "Yeah I understand. I will consider it. It was good to see you."

The Teenage Brained Adults

Theo: Ria! I hear you're coming with us to church tonight. And to get food.

Kehlani: Theo! I told you it was still a maybe, and not to bring it up to her!

Ashton: She did say that, but since the cat's out of the bag, are you going tonight?

    Me: Why was I added to a group chat with y'all?

Kayden: For goodness sake, people let a guy sleep will you? Oh hi, Ria.

    Me: Hello Kayden, will anyone answer why I'm in this chat or not...

Theo: So I can ask you if you're actually going to church tonight. Plus then everyone can just see what you say instead of being told.

Kehlani: I swear I had nothing to do with this.

Kayden: You said at the very beginning that you told us that she might go.

    Me: He's got you there, Lani.

103

Kehlani: *Don't call me Lani. It makes me sound old. But fine, I told them. I was excited. Theo, I'm never telling you anything again since you clearly don't know the meaning of "DON'T BRING IT UP TO HER"*

Me: *Do none of you people have work? Why are you all on?*

Kayden: *I'm self-explanatory since my schedule is chaotic, but answer the question sweetheart. Are you or are you not going to church tonight? And to get food after because of food.*

Theo: *Lani and I are getting food together on break. Why are you on?*

Kehlani: *THEO! What did I just say about calling me Lani?*

Me: *Yes, I'm always down for food. Now going to church though, it's still a maybe. Leaning towards yes, but it depends on how tired I am.*

Kayden: *You can't come get dinner with us if you don't go to church. Jk. I'll buy you an energy drink. Or coffee. Whatever you drink.*

Kehlani: *Yay! Theo would also be saying 'yay', but he's currently almost on the floor laughing at my reaction to him calling me Lani.*

Theo: *You're not scary. Your*

threats only make me laugh. Now
if Adria threatened me, I would be
a little scared.

> **Me**: *Thank you, Theo. You all are*
> *annoying for bugging me. And for*
> *bribing me with food after.*

Theo: *But you love us still.*

> **Me**: *At this moment the only one I*
> *can tolerate is Kayd.*

Kehlani: *Hey! What about me?*

> **Me**: *You started this so no. I'm*
> *going back to work. I'll see you*
> *guys later. Maybe.*

Theo: *YOU LOVE US! Okay, bye.*

Kayden: *Theo. Leave her alone.*
See you.

Kehlani: *Bye!*

Ashton: *I leave for five minutes,*
and you're all losing your minds
and threatening her. I need to go
back to work too. Goodbye.

When I get home from work, I instantly run to take a shower and wash off all the stress of the investigation. As I'm about to lay in my bed, my phone starts ringing.

"Damien, what's up?"

There's shuffling in the mic, "Sorry, I'm at work clocking out. I was wondering if you wanted to go get dinner after I get off?"

To be honest, I briefly consider it as an excuse to bail from having to go out with Kehlani, but I knew I already told everyone I would go. "I would love to, but I already told Kehlani," I paused for a second while considering whether or not to tell him, "That I would go to church with her…"

There is silence on his end for an uncomfortable amount of time. "I can't hear you properly. Let me get in the car and call you back." Damien then hangs up on me.

Oh boy. He thinks he heard me wrong. The phone rings again, and I pick it up.

"Sorry. I've left work. Where are you going again? I don't think I heard you." He says, and I can hear the car running in the background.

I roll my eyes, knowing he can't hear me, "I'm going with Kehlani to her church. You heard me the first time."

"Wha…What? Huh? Why? Is she making you go with her?" *For the love of God.*

"No?" I'm kind of surprised, "Why would she force me to go with her? She's been asking me to go for the last two years and has never forced me. I wanted to go."

I can picture him making a face as he says confused, "Oh don't tell me you're starting to believe in that nonsense. It's just an excuse for people's bad behavior. Do you really want to go listen to someone spout nonsense for a couple of hours?"

"Dude! I just want to see why Kehlani and the others devote their lives to going to church and doing stuff. Besides what if that's just the surface of it, and there's more to the story? I can't just not see what else there is. I mean curiosity killed the cat, but satisfaction brought it back, right? And why not? I have nothing better to do."

"I just gave you an out? Besides, after everything you've seen, how can you still believe that there's someone who cares about all of us? You've been in the worst places in Silver Valley and witnessed just how unfair it is for some kids to be on the streets. What about any of that means there's a God that exists."

I sigh, "Yeah sure you gave me an out for something I want to do. And exactly! I don't know how any of that

106

means that a God exists. That's why I'm going to the service, to find out. It can't hurt. If I decide that none of it is true then it's not true. You can gloat about how you're right then."

"I mean I doubt you're going to find anything that makes sense, but go for it. I'm just telling you straight up right now, it's worthless. But I know I'm not going to change your mind" He knows me dang well. I'm not changing my mind no matter how much he tries to persuade me.

I snicker, "Yeah, nothing you say is going to make me change my mind." I pause, "Look, I'm not expecting to suddenly become a Christian, or even believe anything that I'm told. I just want to see why Kehlani, Kayden, and Theo have gone through hell and back, but still believe their god is good."

"I can answer that because they're ignorant and have had the world handed to them on a silver platter."

I groan internally. *Is he always this insufferable?* "Damien, you don't know them. I don't even know all their stories, but it would be ignorant to say they haven't gone through anything. Kehlani literally went through adoption but had some crap happen to her as a toddler. And Theo had to have gone through something traumatic enough that the Kaisers adopted him."

"You're defending them now? Why? You used to say the same things that I'm saying. What changed?" He's genuinely confused, the annoyance is gone.

I'm kind of annoyed at this point, "Because both Kayden and Kehlani were there with me when I went through the two hardest days of my life. And for some weird reason, they were able to quote something in their Bible. Whatever they said made sense, and it helped. No, I don't believe in whatever crap they were talking about, but during the two hardest moments in my life, one of which I'm in right now, their Bible had something written in it that said their god would give me strength. I want that. I want to not feel like

107

I'm being suffocated all the time."

"Adria, that's just how life is. It always gets better. You don't need some imaginary being to tell you that. I get being in a dark time, just not to the point where you'd go to a religion made up by humans wanting to feel better about themselves."

"Well, then that's your decision. Mine is to go listen to what they have to say before making a decision. After having my mother pass, and having to deal with the Blackthorn shooting, I'm desperate to find something that is a light at the end of the tunnel. Both Kayden and Kehlani have said that there is light in the darkness. I'm done talking about this with you. I'm going to learn. Nothing more."

"Oka...wait. You were the one who dealt with the Blackthorn shooting?"

Grateful for the change in subject I say, "Yeah, I was the one who answered the call."

I'm a little scared as to what Damien will respond with, "You were the one who killed the shooter?"

"Yeah. I guess so. It was an accident. I was aiming for his upper leg the second time."

"How many people died because of the gun?"

I can feel the tears welling up in my eyes at the memory, "Eight. Six are fighting for their lives right now."

"What a tragedy. I can't believe it. I hope that you guys figure out how to use this to prevent similar issues."

Before I can respond, I hear the front door open, "Damien, I have to go. Kehlani just got home. We're leaving soon."

"Okay, stay safe."

Chapter 15

"Adria, start getting ready!" Kehlani yells when she gets home.

As she's taking off her shoes, I start walking towards the living room, and yell back, "Okay! How long do I have?

My best friend looks up at me in surprise, "Wait you're going with us tonight?"

"Yeah. I guess I'm curious and I just need to see what and why you three are so dedicated and faithful to this religion. And what time are we leaving? It's like 5:30 right now." I reply, ignoring the blatant shock on Kehlani's face.

Composing herself, she starts walking to her room, and I follow her, "We have to leave in fifty-five minutes. It starts at seven. Eat a little bit since it doesn't end until eight thirty." She immediately starts fixing her makeup and hair, "Are you going with us to dinner after?"

"Yeah, I'm pretty sure I'll get dinner with y'all. It depends on how tired I feel afterward though. Today was kind of rough."

Kehlani then ushers me off to start getting ready, so I head to the kitchen to find a snack. Grabbing an apple, my thoughts start running around. Why am I going to their church? I don't know. I would've never gone, so I'm not sure why I changed my mind. I do wonder what will happen later

109

though. Probably nothing.

I got up once I had finished eating to go get ready. Running to my room, I put on a fresh outfit, and redo my makeup. As I'm spraying the setting spray, Kehlani calls out, "Adria! We have to leave soon! Hurry up!"

"I'm coming!" I yell back as I'm fixing the white collar peeking out of my navy sweatshirt in the mirror.

Grabbing my bag, I run to the door to put on my shoes. "Ooooh. I like the baggy blue jeans." Kehlani compliments. I pause for a minute knowing she'll continue. Recognition hits her face, "Wait… Are those mine?

I smile innocently as I stand up, "I have no idea what you're talking about. Now let's go, I thought you said we had to leave."

Shaking her head at my response, Kehlani leads me out the door. It takes us around fifteen minutes to get to the church

Is this something I genuinely want to do?

Somehow Kehlani can sense my thoughts or something, "Adria! I swear if you're thinking of backing out it's too late. We're already here. Just try it okay? I can't promise anything, but it'll answer some of the questions you have okay."

I roll my eyes dramatically but follow her out of the car and into the sanctuary. As I scan the room, it seems like the room can fit a couple hundred people. We look around for our friends who are saving our seats. Quickly we found them, and all three of them got up to come meet us by the door.

Everyone says hi to each other, and as Kehlani, Theo, and Ashton start walking to where the boys are sitting, Kayden falls back to walk with me.

He holds up a cup that I only just noticed he is holding, "You know, Kehlani tells me that you're tired, and we can't have you falling asleep while Pastor Jason is teaching."

"What is it?" I question, a little suspicious.

Kayden laughs, "I'm not trying to poison you, I promise. It's only coffee. You said that you would need caffeine to stay awake, so I brought you some."

"I still don't trust you, but I need caffeine so I'll drink it," I say with a grin.

"So how are you?"

I answer a bit stiffly, "Surprised I'm here, but if you're asking how I'm feeling after Monday. I don't have an answer for you." I scoff, "Heck, I don't even have an answer for myself."

When we sit down, we all talk for a couple of minutes before the lights dim, and music starts to play. My friends begin to stand up, and I follow their lead. *What's going on and why is everyone standing*

The woman on the small stage starts singing, and I hear Kehlani and Kayden start singing along. *The music is nice. Not sure what it's for, but it's nice.* I decide to just sway to the music.

> *There is another in the fire*
> *Standing next to me*
> *There is another in the waters*
> *Holding back the seas*
> *And should I ever need reminding*
> *What power set me free*
> *There is a grave that holds nobody*
> *Now that power lives in me*

The lyrics catch me off guard. I'm not sure what to make of the words that everyone is singing

> *Nothing stands between us*
> *There'll be another in the fire*
> *Standing next to me*

111

There'll be another in the waters
Holding back the seas
And should I ever need reminding
What power set me free
There is a grave that holds nobody
Now that power lives in me.

When the song ends, Kayden looks over at me and asks, "Hey, you okay?"

To be honest with you, I didn't know what to think. I am frozen in place for a second. "Uh." Snapping out of it, "Sorry, yeah. I'm fine. It just caught me off guard. I'm good though."

I can tell Kayden knows there's more than what I told him, but thankfully, he doesn't press and just turns back to the stage to sing along with the next song.

Set me free? Standing in the fire with me? Although there's another song playing, the lyrics of the last one continues to replay in my brain.

When the song ends, we all sit down, and the pastor comes out and immediately starts teaching.

"Okay, everyone. We're going to be studying First John chapter one verses eight through ten. Get out your Bibles, and let us pray."

Kehlani hands me a Bible opened to the passage that he had just said we would be studying. She then bows her head and closes her eyes, motioning for me to do the same.

"Dear Heavenly Father, today's study is focusing on the effects of your sacrifice. Deception is running rampant in our current world, and I pray that You would just lift the veil of deception that the enemy has placed in the hopes that we would turn away from You. For those who do not know You yet, would You give them clarity, and understanding, so that they may turn to You? God, I pray that You would use me to preach to this congregation. And in Jesus' name, I pray." He

112

pauses as the congregation, as a whole, closes out his prayer.

How the heck does he know it's my first time here? Did he know or is this a coincidence?

I look down to read the passage as Pastor Jason, I think that is his name, reads it out loud.

He is faithful and just to forgive us of our sins. I reread that, and I cannot understand it. *Cleanse us from all unrighteousness.* None of this makes sense, but I continue to read and listen to the pastor speak.

"Look, with several hundred people in this room there are chances that some of the mistakes you've made were impactful in others' lives. There's no doubt that without God, you are holding on to that guilt, but you don't need to. Being a Christian doesn't mean that we no longer make mistakes, or that suddenly we're perfect. It means that the mistakes we make are forgiven. And in no way does that mean 'Oh if I'm a Christian so I can go out and murder someone for no reason, it's okay, God forgives me.' Being Christian means that slowly we are transformed to be more like Christ."

Okay, now this is freaking me out. Is he reading my mind right now? Did Kehlani tell him that I was coming or something and this is what I wanted answers to? What is going on?

"Galatians 2:20 says 'I have been crucified with Christ; it is no longer I who live, but Christ lives in me; and the life which I now live in the flesh I live by faith in the Son of God who loved me and gave Himself for me.' By living as His people, and following His rules, we start to naturally become more like Him. We are to imitate Him. Paul said in 1st Corinthians 11:1 'Imitate me, just as I imitate Christ.'"

I know it doesn't make sense, but the words he is saying are overwhelming my brain, and I can't stay here. "Hey, sorry I need to use the restroom." Both Kayden and Ashton move their legs so I can leave.

I walk quickly to the bathroom, wanting to get out of

here as quickly as possible. *This is too much.*

Once I finish using the restroom, I sit on a bench in the foyer, not ready to go back in. *How did he know about the guilt?*

After a bit of time, a deep voice from the hallway scares me, "Adria? Are you okay?"

My head pops up at the sound of my name. When I see it's Kayden, I sigh and answer, "Yeah, Kayd. I'm here. I just really don't want to go back in right now."

He walks over, sitting down next to me, and joins me staring at the ceiling. "So, is there something wrong? I know that everything you're hearing is new to you, but what made you leave?"

I don't want to tell him the truth, because it will make it real. "Nothing. I just thought what he was saying was absolute crap. I don't need to listen to it anymore. There's nothing more to it." I lie smoothly.

Kayden raises his eyebrows in response. "Mhm. Nice lie. But now do you want to try telling the truth?"

"How do you know I wasn't telling the truth?"

He smirks, "Because when you actually believe that what you're hearing is crap, you've got more force behind your words. You sound exhausted right now. If you truly believed what he was saying was crap, you'd be a little more excited that you were right."

I groan, "How do you know when I do stuff like that?" I decide to tell him the truth, "I just... You're the last person I was going to tell you this, but whatever. What he said was so personal. It sounded like he was calling me out."

Kayden looks confused at my complaining, "But everything he said was so generic. All he mentioned was deception, new Christians, guilt, and living in the footsteps of God." Understanding crosses his face, "It was guilt. The shooting. That's the whole reason you decided to give Christianity a chance."

114

"Yeah." I sigh, "This is so stupid. Why am I so upset over someone's opinion? But how did he know that I was new to church, or even the mistake thing?"

"Because you know he's right. Your soul knows it, but your flesh doesn't want to accept it. A soul that was created by God in his image, versus the fallen flesh that wants to disobey him. And that's a choice that you need to make."

I stare at Kayden like he has two heads, "What are you talking about? Flesh versus soul?"

'For all have sinned and fallen short of the glory of God.' God gave us a choice when He placed Adam and Eve in the garden. God had given them the Garden of Eden to do what they wanted, and their only rule was to not eat from the Tree of the Knowledge of Good and Evil. And can you guess what they did?

The question had an obvious answer, "Ate from the tree." I answer.

Kayden fake applauds, "Yet. And now, we all sin, which means eternal damnation. Because God is perfect, He cannot sin. For Him to accept us as we are means He isn't perfect and doesn't have perfect standards."

I nod along as he continues, "But luckily for us, that wasn't the end of the story. Around four thousand years later, He sent a rescue plan. Jesus, God's only Son was both one hundred percent God and one hundred percent man. He lived the perfect life that we couldn't. He lived without sin. He was then falsely accused then killed for blasphemy. Thankfully, He didn't stay dead. He rose from the dead, and is still alive to this day."

Kayden's face has excitement and joy written all over it. "The perfect blood that was spilled was the salvation for all of us. The way for us to go to heaven instead of hell. That is the reason Kehlani, Theo, Ashton, and I still have hope. We know where we're going in the end."

It makes sense, but I still ask, "Then why live with

so much joy on Earth? Wouldn't it be better to die than go to heaven?"

I half expect him to laugh at me, but he doesn't. "Our mission while we're here is to bring others to that understanding too. To accept the gift that Jesus has given us."

"But then if he died for everyone, why don't we all go to heaven? Why do we have to believe he died and rose again? Doesn't that make the gift only for specific people? Like, I don't know if my parents accepted him. If they didn't, are they in hell?"

Kayden stops for a minute, and then says, "Let's put it this way, if you receive a gift, and never open it or use it, will it do anything for you?"

I think for a moment, and say, "No, it does nothing. I need to know what it is, or open it for it to work."

"As for your parents, I don't know. That commitment is between them and God"

I'm disappointed, but I suppose it makes sense. All I can do is hope that they've made it to heaven. I think for a moment.

"But why would He die? I mean it's common knowledge that He was crucified, and the Romans were anything but gracious. There's no way it was a painless death." My face scrunches up in confusion,

"Love." I still don't get it, so he continues, "He loved us that much, that he was willing to die for three days, and be separated from God to make sure that anyone who believed in Him would be able to return to heaven and live with Him forever."

Everything kind of clicks into place, "Oh my gosh..."

Kayden smiles and nods, "Yep. That was my reaction too."

People then start filing out of the sanctuary, "Come on, let's go find our friends. It looks like they're done."

Before I get up, I say, "Thank you." He looks a little confused, so I elaborate, "Thank you for coming out to make sure I was okay, and for answering my questions."

Kayden grins and holds his hand out to help me up from the bench. *Holy crap he has dimples.* "Glad I could help. Text me if you need anything, even if you think it's stupid because chances are it's not. You're on the right track, and so close to the truth, you just need to believe it."

Chapter 16

"Adria! Come on, we're going to get some food. I'm hungry." Kehlani yells to me as we walk over to our group of friends.

I jog over to her, and say, "Let's go. I'm going to die of hunger if we don't get food anytime soon. If we don't go soon I'm going to pass out, and you're going to have to take me home."

It is evident that she is surprised. She definitely did not expect me to want to come. "Dramatic much? You ate before we left and you had food. If you pass out though, whether fake or not, I'm not taking you home. I'll make Kayden or Ashton carry you home. I don't work out enough for that."

"Why Kayden or Ashton, and not Theo."

She gives me a pointed look, and I already know the answer, "Out of the three of them is Theo the one you would trust the most to carry you."

I snicker, "You're right. He'd start carrying me, get distracted, forget he's carrying me then drop me."

"I'm right here you know!" Theo protests, and Kehlani and I burst into a fit of giggles.

"Are we wrong?" I ask.

Instead of Theo answering, Ashton does instead,

119

"You are not. He would one hundred percent drop you if he got distracted."

Theo looks offended, then picks up Kehlani and throws her over his shoulder, "I'll show you guys that I won't drop her." He yells out as he runs out of the church.

"Is anyone else worried she's going to hurt herself?" I question once the two are out of sight.

Both Kayden and Ashton shrug. "I think we're past the point of worrying about those two. They'll survive. Plus Kehlani's a middle school teacher. She'll be fine." Ashton replies calmly. *Is this a normal thing?*

The three of us talk for a couple of minutes until both Theo and Kehlani return. As they're walking towards us, I hear her scolding him. I turn to Kayden and Ashton, "Ten bucks he dropped her."

"I'm not taking that bet. I'm on your side. I think that he dropped her," Kayden declines. Ashton nods in agreement.

Kehlani huffs towards me, and says, "The idiot lost his balance, and started to trip. I nearly fell on my face. At least I was wearing a t-shirt and jeans this time instead of a dress." She's now full-on glaring at Theo who looks extremely sheepish.

"Kiki, I'm sorry. It was an accident. I was looking up at the lights, and I didn't mean to. I caught you before you hit the ground." Theo apologizes sporting puppy dog eyes.

Now normally, Kehlani would forgive him right away, but he's just called her Kiki. Not sure how she feels about that nickname right after he just dropped her, to be honest.

As the two are bickering, Kayden, Ashton, and I figure out where we want to eat. Once it's decided, we split apart the bickering friends and head to the diner we found.

120

Rat. Tap. Tap. Both Kehlani and I jump. Kehlani screams, and I pull out a pocket knife and hold it out towards the door.

A muffled voice from outside says, "Chill, you two. It's just me." *Oh, he is going to get it.*

Kehlani instantly gets out of the car and yells at Theo, "I'm going to kill you later!"

Kayden and Ashton walk over and stop when they witness Kehlani scolding Theo. Kayden is the first to speak, "What did my brother do to get Kehlani to lose it on him? Other than dropping her earlier of course."

"He was tapping on our window when we parked and she got scared."

Ashton laughs as Kayden walks over to Theo, and smacks him in the head. "Ouch!"

We start to walk into the diner. "No screams from you I see, Ms. Police Officer," Ashton remarks.

I snort, "Yeah, well if I screamed every time something scared me, I wouldn't be alive right now. Don't tell Theo that he did scare me. His ego would go through the roof, and I don't want to deal with that right now."

"I can't disagree with that. On a completely different topic though, are you okay?" *Sudden change in conversation, but okay.*

"Yes, I'm fine." He opens the door for me, "Thank you. I'm okay. Go tell the other two that I'm fine, so y'all will stop asking."

Ashton rolls his eyes. *Sassy.* "We only ask if you're okay because we care about you." And then as if he knows what I'm thinking, he continues, "You can think we don't care, but we do. You're one of our friends. Of course, we're going to make sure you're okay."

I chuckle a little and sigh, "Why are you all so nice?

I genuinely don't think the four of you have been mean a day in your lives."

"It's interesting you think that because there's no way that's true. We all have our moments, but we try not to. The Bible says to deny the flesh that wants us to sin, and that's what we strive to do every day." He explains as we sit down.

Once we order, everyone starts talking. I kind of sit back and listen. Eventually, though, Theo speaks up, "So, Ria are you going to go with us to church now?"

"I wouldn't be opposed to going again, considering I left halfway through this time. I won't make any promises though." I say. Kehlani is clearly surprised, but Kayden smiles knowingly.

"Oh joy, I'll have two women constantly being mean to me instead of just one now." Theo says teasingly."

"I'm not mean! You deserve everything that happens to you. Adria though on the other hand." Kehlani defends while throwing me under the bus.

All of us turn to her in disbelief, "Okay, fine. Maybe I do say some out-of-pocket things. But you guys start it."

Theo retorts, "We're dudes. That in itself is already an excuse for our actions. What about you? You're supposed to be a lady."

"I'm a police officer. I don't do nice, or sugarcoating." I retort.

As we're arguing, Kayden cuts in, "Okay children. You can stop arguing about the reasons you both enjoy acting like children."

I snort, "Says the man-child himself. You do all the things you're accusing him and me of."

Kehlani laughs and says, "Kayd, I think she's got you there."

The five of us continue talking and laughing throughout our dinner.

"Kayden!" We all yell when we find out that he paid

122

the bill. Kayden just shrugs and gives us an innocent smile.

As we're getting up to leave, Kehlani comes up to me, and she's sporting puppy-dog eyes. I sigh, "What are you going to ask me that I'm going to regret saying yes to?"

"I can never fool you. Can I borrow your car so Theo and I can go out for a little? Please?" Kehlani begs.

I roll my eyes, "And how am I going to get home?"

"Kayden can take you home." She suggests.

I sigh, "If Kayden's okay with it, then sure, I'll go with him. You're lucky I don't have to work tomorrow."

"Thank you! Thank you! Thank you!" She squeals and hugs me. I give her a half-hearted one back.

When she runs off to tell Theo, I yell to Kayd, "Kayden! It looks like I'm going home with you so our best friends can go make out." The four of them give me a look, "Fine, I'm joking about the making out part. But I do need you to take me home. Can we go? I want to sleep."

"Do you want something to drink?" Kayden asks.

I sigh at the situation, "Yeah, sure. Can I have a Dr. Pepper?"

"Yeah, I'll get it. I'm guessing from your sigh that neither Kehlani nor Theo has responded to tell you when they're getting home?" Kayden laughs as he gets me the drink I asked for.

"Yep. Although I guess it's my fault that I forgot my house key."

"Okay well, you just sit there, I'm going to go change out of the clothes I've been wearing since I got off work. If you want me to find you something to change into, I can." Kayden suggests.

"It's fine, the sweater's comfortable. I'll wait here." I assure him as he walks into his room.

The silence offers me a moment to just sit and think about everything they talked about at church. *I think it makes sense. But what if it's not real?*

After sitting, and waiting for a little bit, I decide to get up and walk around the house. My thoughts are still running through my mind. When I get to the living room, a large book catches my eye. *Why's there so much color bleeding out of the side of the pages?* I grab the book and flip through the pages full of highlighted sentences. A highlighted, and underlined sentence catches my eye, and I abruptly stop flipping through the pages. *"Exhorting them to continue in their faith, and saying, 'We must through many tribulations enter the kingdom of God.'"* Notes in the little margin of the book are, *"It is a human instinct when discouraged to turn to its Creator, and many times, we are put in those tribulations to seek Him."*

"I see you found my old Bible," Kayden says, scaring me when he walks up behind me.

I turn around while still holding the Bible. "What does this mean?" I ask while showing him the verse.

"The note or the verse?"

"Both."

Kayden nods and says, "Okay the verse was essentially Paul encouraging the current-day Christians to keep up their faith. Being Christian was never supposed to be all rainbows and sunshine. Jesus even said that because the world hated Him first, they would hate us also. But the point is that the tribulations and issues are what help shape us and continue to grow in the Lord, hence the 'enter the kingdom of God.'"

I nod along, and he continues, "Now the note part. What's usually the first thing you say when you're in danger?"

I thought for a moment, "Oh my God, help me..."

"Mhm, and if you don't mind me using your current

situation as an example, you didn't care for God up until things got hard. Being in a difficult place softens your heart, and you are more open to listening to us. Now you're asking the right questions."

We both pause and sit in silence for a couple minutes, as I'm sorting through my thoughts. I open my mouth to say something but ultimately decide not to say anything.

Kayden notices my hesitancy and asks, "What is it, sweetheart."

I'm honestly surprised that he noticed something is off, "It's nothing."

He rolls his eyes at my refusal to say anything, "Just tell me. I can tell that you think the question is stupid, but when it comes to God, there really are no stupid questions. So ask away."

I relent and say, "But are there things that are unforgivable, if so, then I've definitely done the unforgivable thing."

Sympathy covers Kayden's face "Look at me. There is one and only one unforgivable sin that is mentioned in the Bible, and you're not committing that sin right now. Matthew 12:31 says, 'Therefore I say to you, every sin and blasphemy will be forgiven men, but blasphemy against the Spirit will not be forgiven men.' Now that is the only unforgivable sin, and the fact that you're asking me questions about God shows me that you haven't committed that sin yet."

"Adria, Kehlani, and I are only constantly trying to tell you about God because we want you to experience the joy that we have experienced. Not just that but also the fact that if you choose to continue living a life without God, your eternal destination would be hell, and none of us want that for you."

I sigh and stare at the Bible in my hands, "I don't know okay. I really don't. It sounds very interesting, but it's just not that easy to take such a blind leap of faith. Thank you

125

for providing clarity."

"No problem." He smiles.

I look up at him and return the smile. *Oh goodness, his dimples.*

Ding. I check my phone, and I see a message from Kehlani saying that she has gotten home, so she can let me in. She also apologizes for not seeing my message.

"Kehlani?" Kayden asks.

"Yep. I'm gonna go home now, but thank you for the drink, and hanging out with me for a bit. Oh, and for answering my questions. It helped, sorry I couldn't completely commit to it yet." I reply.

Kayden hugs me. It catches me off guard, but once I shake myself out of surprise, I return the hug. "You don't need to worry about it. And making that decision is something you have to do on your own time. I can't force you to do anything. It's a choice. But if you have any other questions or concerns, just call me okay?"

"I will."

Chapter 17

"Adria! I know you just got home. There's a package on the table for you. It got here like an hour ago." Kehlani yells when I walk through the door.

I am surprised that anyone is home, "Why are you home so early? I was supposed to be back first today!"

Kehlani walks out of her room still fully dressed from her day at work, "They had a half day for the junior highers. I don't know why but any day I can take a break from those pre-hormonal children I will take."

I shake my head at her answer. *She would be the type to both love and hate her students.* I grab the box cutter and start opening my box.

Kehlani peeks over my shoulder and asks, "So what did you order this time?"

I think for a moment because I honestly don't remember ordering anything, "Wait, I didn't order anything..." I quicken my movements to open the package. When I open the package, two words stare back at me. *Holy Bible.* I look at Kehlani and ask, "Did you get this for me?"

We're both just as confused as each other, "No? If I wanted to give you a Bible, I would've just given you one of the several I have."

I take the Bible out of the box and look for the receipt.

Oh my goodness. He did not. I stare at the slip for a little longer, and burst into laughter, "He didn't."

"He did what? Who did this? I'm confused. Why are you laughing?" Kehlani asks, still visibly puzzled.

I hand her the slip of paper, "Look, here's the gift receipt."

Kehlani's eyes scan over the paper, and when she sees the name, realization crosses her face, "Oh my goodness. It was Kayden. Why am I not surprised? What's with the note under it?"

"There's a note?" I rummage through the box one more time before finding the note. *Hope you like the gift sweetheart. Just so you can note down anything you want to remember.* "Oh wow." I'm extremely surprised by this. "Kehlani, is this normal?"

"The gift giving? I don't know, I just think that gift-giving is Kayden's form of affection. It's a way he can 'serve others' in a sense."

"No, I mean giving me a Bible."

"Oh no, not really. He wanted you to have a Bible so you could continue studying and learning about Jesus. If you hadn't gotten a Bible by the next time you went with us to church, I'm positive you would've had one by the next time." she explains.

As she's talking, I'm still staring at the leather-bound Bible. As my hand runs through the spine, a small dip catches my attention. *Adria Juliette Sousa.* "Oh my goodness! He got my name engraved on the spine."

The Bible is no longer in my hands as Kehlani snatches it. She stares at the book in disbelief, "Oh my gosh. He didn't."

"Is he always like this? How is anyone even this nice? Or considerate? And why did he even get my name engraved on the Bible." The rapid-fire questions come out of my mouth.

Kehlani just shrugs, "I have no idea. Well, yes he's always this nice. Why he did it though, there are two answers to that. Either one he saw the option and thought, 'Oh why not.' or he's just spent enough time with Brooklyn to know that engravings are something girls like."

I don't know how to respond to that, and I don't want to hear the second option, so I change the subject, "I'm going to put this in my room, shower quickly, and then you want to go out to go get dinner?"

When she nods, I quickly run to my room. As soon as the door closes, I finally have a moment to think. *This man actually bought me a Bible and had my name engraved onto it.*

> *Me: Kayden, are you joking with me right now?*
> *Kayden: What did I do, sweetheart?*
> *Me: Well for one you're calling me sweetheart, but the other thing is, really? You got me a Bible? Why?*
> *Kayden: Oh, I thought you were actually mad. Do you not like it?*
> *Me: Sorry, I realize I sound ungrateful. Thank you for the gift, but what on earth possessed you to want to get something like this for me?*
> *Kayden: Uh, the Bible was a nice, black one that kind of looked like the one at my house two days ago, and I thought you would like it?*
> *Me: And the name engraving?*
> *Kayden: It's your first Bible. Why not make it memorable?*

129

Me: *This is too much. There's no way that getting it engraved would've been cheap. Not to mention you had this delivered in less than two days.*

Kayden: *It's called a gift for a reason. But in all seriousness, there's nothing more to it. I want that Bible to have meaning to you. I want you to read it, and hopefully grow closer to God. Just take it okay?*

Me: *I cannot believe you... But thank you. I will hurt you the next time I see you because this was too much, but thank you for the Bible. I will try and read it soon.*

Kayden: *You're welcome. I suggest starting with John, but if you want help starting, we could always do a study together.*

Adria: *I might take you up on that. But I've got to go for now. I'll let you know. Thanks again.*

Putting my phone away, I quickly run to take a shower and change into a brown hoodie and jeans. When I'm finished, Kehlani and I head out to get dinner.

Once we get to the restaurant, and order, the interrogations begin. Kehlani does not hesitate to start asking me about the gift, "What happened with you and Kayden on Wednesday that convinced him to buy you a Bible?"

"Uhm. We may or may not have had two very long conversations about Jesus. I don't know, my mentality just changed overnight, and I think he thought that giving me a

Bible would convince me not to give up on it, or dismiss any of the questions I had." I admit

Kehlani sighs, "Of course he did. But he's not wrong though." I nod in agreement as she continues, "Kayden's extremely intelligent and knows how people think."

"He wasn't wrong in this case. He did tell me to read John first?" I say.

"Yeah. It's where new believers usually start. Knowing him, he probably offered to read it with you." I nod to confirm, "I mean, if you're considering it, I'd say go for it. Kayden's gotten you to understand the Bible and its meanings more in-depth than I have. When you do, give your heart to Christ,"

I make a face at her last sentence and Kehlani rolls her eyes, "Adria, you've already gone to church, and you want to learn more about Christ, it's a possibility."

I stop my look of disgust as I realize she's right. "Now I'm going to say, in the beginning, sure do a study with Kayden, but later on I suggest doing it with another female because she's going to help you grow faster than a male would. But for now, I say go for it."

The more I think about it, the more I think she's right, so I agree and take my phone out to text Kayden.

>**Me**: *Yeah let's do it. Can we start tomorrow?*
>
>**Kayden**: *Yeah. We can start tomorrow. Just read a chapter a day, and we'll meet like once a week, or every other week so we can talk about it and ask questions. Do you want to meet on Sunday after church so we can*

talk about it?

> *Me: Yeah sure. I don't think I'm going to go to church on Sunday though. We'll see how I'm feeling. I'm down to go to lunch after though.*
>
> *Kayden: I won't pressure you, but I do hope you'll change your mind, and go. Sounds good though. Goodnight Adria.*
>
> *Me: Goodnight Kayden. Thank you.*

Yawn. I get up to check my phone, only to realize it is almost eleven. *Geez I slept in late. I didn't even work the Saturday night shift.* Kayden and I had made plans to meet up at the coffee shop around two. Kehlani had already left for church, which meant I had enough time to shower and get ready.

After a slower morning, I check my outfit in the mirror and change a couple of times before deciding on baggy jeans, a black top, and a racing bomber jacket. I grab my keys and run out the door.

Before walking into the coffee shops, I contemplate backing out for a second. *Since when did I start caring about this Jesus stuff? To be honest, I don't know, but it puts my mind at ease.* Eventually, I decide that I want to do this.

I ordered my coffee, before sitting down to wait for Kayden. *2:15. Where is he?*

"Hey, sorry. Have you been waiting long?" I shake my head. "Okay, that's good. Did you get your coffee yet?"

"Yeah, I did, so just order yours." I give him an innocent look, "And if mine just so happens to come out while you're there, can you get it for me?"

Kayden chuckles, "I'll get you your coffee if it's out. I'll be right back."

When he comes back, not only is he holding a coffee, but he also brings two small sandwiches. He hands me both the coffee and a sandwich. I give him a look.

"Have you eaten yet?" When I shake my head, he smirks, "So eat."

"You didn't need to buy me a sandwich. I was going to eat once we finished." I try to argue.

Kayden rolls his eyes, "Just eat it. I already bought it."

We go back and forth for a couple minutes, before I relent, and resign to eating the sandwich. When Kayden's coffee arrives, we both take out our Bibles.

Kayden decides to start, "Okay, let's start with notes from chapter one, and then move on to questions." I agree and he continues, "What was the biggest thing you noticed?"

I flip through the pages of the Bible, and when I find the page I am looking for, I scan through the highlights and notes. "I think verse fourteen made me think. It says that the Word became flesh, and we beheld His glory. In the end, Jesus started calling over His followers, and they dropped everything they knew to go with Him. That kind of surprises me."

Kayden asks a follow-up question, "Two questions, who is the Word? And what surprised you? That they dropped everything to follow Jesus?"

I stop to think for a moment, "Is Jesus the Word?" he nods, impressed, and I continue, "I think it surprised me that they dropped everything just to go follow Jesus. Do you think they knew that He was God?"

Kayden answers me, "I don't think they knew that He was the Messiah because, in a future chapter, Jesus asks His disciples, 'Who do you think I am?' The only one who

133

said that He was God was Peter."

"So then why would they drop everything to follow some guy that they knew nothing about?"

"What do you think that reason is?" Kayden counters.

I don't know. That's why I'm asking you. I stop for a second, "Is it possible that although they didn't know that he was God, they could tell that there was something different about him?"

Kayden smiles, "Yeah, I think so too."

He's still smiling, "Why are you still smiling?"

"You're not talking about the Bible as if it's a maybe, but rather as if it's true. When did that change?"

I freeze when I realize that he's right, "Maybe I have started realizing that the Bible is true, or at least considering the possibility that it is true."

"That's amazing. I hope that you continue to walk towards that path."

We finish discussing the chapter, and I surprisingly had a very nice time with Kayden. Once we finish up at the coffee shop, Kayden and I decide to go walk around at the Blackthorn Mall. To be honest, when I first got there, the memories of the shooting last week caught me off guard. Thankfully, Kayden just talked me through it, and we spent the rest of the afternoon hanging out.

For the next month, I continue to read through the book of John. Kayden and I would continue to meet up either Sunday after church or Wednesday before church. I didn't go every single time to service, but I did go as often as I could. Each time I went, my mindset against Christianity became softer.

Chapter 18

"Ria! Hi!" Ellie yells when I Facetime her. "Charlie! Come here and say hi to Adria!"

At the call, Charlotte comes running over and jumps on top of Ellie who yelps and steals the phone. "Hey, Ria!"

"Hey, you two. How was your birthday weekend? I'm sorry I didn't get to go up to Roseburrough." I apologize.

The girls start talking over each other trying to tell me how their weekend with their friends went. I gather that they went to the mall, and had cake with Avó and Vovô but that's about it.

Afterward, the three of us talk about how they were coping, and adjusting to living with Avó and Vovô. Charlotte seems to be doing well, and adjusting well. I've been texting her, and I think her friends have helped talk her through it.

Elianna on the other hand still seems to be struggling. I can tell that something is still wrong. She's been much quieter, and her sparkle has faded so much. It breaks me to see her lose the enthusiasm that made her, well, her.

Charlie has to go, as she and her friend are about to head out. When she leaves, Ellie and I continue to talk.

"Did Brooklyn ever get back to you when I gave you her number?"

Ellie nods, "Yeah, she did. She's nice and cool. I

cannot wait until I graduate high school, and get to go to college"

I snicker, "Yep. She's basically the coolest person I've ever met, besides Kehlani. Did she talk to you about Mom?"

"Mhm. We talked for a bit, but she still keeps up with me. It's helped a lot, and I've gotten through it." Ellie sighs. There's something still off, but I let it slide.

We talk about school. She gives me all the latest gossip about her friends, and I seriously forgot how much drama being in school is.

The way she describes her friends worries me. Charlie's friends helped her through Mom's passing, but Ellie's friends haven't seemed to do much for her. I don't love the things they talk about or the way they act, but I've never met any of them. Plus, knowing Ellie, the more I tell her not to do something, the more she'll want to do it.

"So, how's Kayden?" Ellie asks, abruptly changing the subject.

I freeze, "Why, what has Kehlani told you?"

"Oh, so something is happening…"

Dang it. Why'd I have to react like that? "No… there is not. I thought that Kehlani would have exaggerated us hanging out."

Ellie's grin grows, "Oh, so you're hanging out now. I thought that y'all were barely friends."

I roll my eyes, "We're friends now. Nothing else. Leave it be."

"Adria! Come on, we're going to be late." Damien yells.

I pop my head out the door, my makeup half-done. "I got home from work forty-five minutes ago. Leave me alone for a bit. Also, we're going to get dinner, why are we going to be late? It's Tuesday, no one's going out."

"Well I'm hungry, and we both know you didn't eat at work today." He counters.

I roll my eyes and yell from my room, "Well maybe if you texted me first instead of just showing up at my house, you wouldn't have to wait so long."

Damien snorts, "And be bored at home? I'd rather bug you."

"The more you bug me, the longer I will take out of spite. So keep it up, and I will take longer." I threaten. Damien is silent, so I go back to getting ready. Eventually, we do end up leaving to go get dinner.

Usually, whenever we hang out, we avoid the topic of my job, since we tend to not see eye to eye, but tonight is different. "So how have you been after having to deal with the shooting?"

It has been a month, and in complete actuality, for a couple of weeks, I have blocked the memory from my mind. After Kayden advised me to speak to his father about it. I took his advice and I regained the memories and dealt with the guilt.

"Yeah, I've been doing a lot better. I spoke to Chief Kaiser about the guilt, and he helped me through it." I answer.

"Does that mean you've hung out with those Jesus freaks too?" he snickers.

I roll my eyes, "No of course not." *Why did I just lie? What's the purpose of that?*

Damien continues, "Well after that disaster, I hope you and the rest of the station will start to support the new California gun law. It would be beneficial if Chief Kaiser announced his support for the bill."

I freeze, "Support gun bans? I'm hoping that is not what you mean."

"Yeah, I'm talking about gun bans. What else would

137

I mean?" He asks, confused.

I snort, "I would never support a gun ban. Do you realize you're talking to a police officer?"

"Exactly, you've literally seen firsthand how guns can affect our community in a negative way." He explains as if that will change my mind.

I'm livid now, "And yet I had to use a gun to stop the Blackthorn shooter. Would you rather I had left him, and he hurt more people than he did?"

"If the gun ban was a law, he wouldn't have the gun in the first place. None of this would've happened."

"The person was mentally insane. He wanted to shoot up the mall for God knows what reason. Even if guns were banned, he would've found a way to find one. Think about it."

We're both fired up now, "Adria..."

"No! Don't even start. Did you know that there have been some calls where I showed up and the shooter had already been detained? Do you know who stopped the shooter? Yeah, someone who owned a gun. Yes, guns can be harmful, but that's only if they're put in the hands of someone who isn't mentally sane."

I pick up a butter knife sitting at the table, "If the knife is on the table, does it do anything?" He shakes his head. "Exactly, the knife will only do harm if the person using it has the intent of harm."

"That's a completely different scenario," He argues, "Guns do so much more harm than good. You got to the shooting scene within fifteen minutes, and the shooter still killed eight people, six of which were critically injured, and are lucky to be alive. Wouldn't you rather lessen the risk of him having the gun?"

"You're not listening to me! No! No, I wouldn't like to restrict the use of a firearm. No matter how many laws you place, you're not going to stop someone who's *mentally insane* from using one." I return.

Damien rolls his eyes, and says, "Wow, I thought you were different. Hanging out with those Christianity people has really changed you."

I scoff, "Yeah, well I guess they make better friends than you do, considering you don't even listen to me."

"So you admit you do hang out with them, including at their church. You're already lying to me." He attacks.

I'm so over this fight, "Because I knew you would react like this. Enough. I'm done arguing with you. I'm sorry for lying, but I'm not sorry for what I believe in."

"So you're one of them now?" He asks in disbelief.

I haven't given it much thought until now, and maybe some of my answers were out of spite, but I say, "Yeah, I guess I am. I do believe in a God, and that God saved me."

"I did not think you were going to give into a bunch of made-up crap that was told to make people feel better."

I'm at my breaking point, "Stop! Just stop. Let me live my life without you judging and butting in. I let you live yours with your own beliefs. I may not agree with them, but I don't tell you that you're an idiot for believing in them."

Anger flares up in Damien's face again, "They've judged us since we met them, telling us we're 'sinful'. But when I do it, I'm the bad guy. Have you actually let them brainwash you into believing in their religion?"

"They didn't approve of us living without Christ, but they never butted in, or got angry over it. You've only yelled at me since I told you I started going to church. Not once has any of them yelled at me for not believing in God. They did the opposite. They just shared their beliefs whenever they could, when it was appropriate." I defend.

Damien snorts, "Fine. If they're such great people, why don't you go back to them tonight."

My anger has reached its limits, "Sounds good." I toss a twenty-dollar bill on the table. "Use this to pay for my

139

dinner. I'm not sitting here just to spend the rest of my night arguing with you." With that, I walk out of the restaurant and head home.

Kayden: I have to work before church, so we can't meet before then. I'm sorry.

> *Me: Yeah, that's fine. I'm not really in the mood to go out to be completely honest with you.*

Kayden: And now, I can't not ask. What happened? Why are you upset?

> *Me: Are you ever not stupidly nice?*

Kayden: Is it stupidly nice to want to ask why my friend got upset and seems to be upset?

> *Me: No, I guess. Sorry, I'm tired and slightly annoyed with someone.*

Kayden: Fight? With Damien, I'd assume? Before you ask, Kehlani's with Theo, you wouldn't have fought with her.

> *Me: Does everyone think that they're my only two friends?*

Kayden: No. Well, yes. But Theo's here so I doubt he did anything, and you're talking to me so I'm good. And Ashton is too good for anyone to ever be mad at him. So the only other person could only be Damien.

> **Me**: *Fine, yes. We fought, and we both got pissed. I walked out of our dinner because I got that upset.*

Kayden: *What happened then?*

> **Me**: *Me going to church, hanging out with you, and being against gun bans.*

Kayden: *Were you completely innocent? Or did you egg him on too?*

> **Me**: *Why are you asking me? He's the one who started it, and I defended my position.*

Kayden: *Because you're a witness. Look, if you're talking to an unbeliever about Christ, but you're yelling at them, they're not going to take anything from what you're trying to show them.*

> **Me**: *Does that mean I need to apologize to him?*

Kayden: *I won't tell you the answer, but I think you should.*

> **Me**: *Fine. Maybe. We'll see.*

Kayden: *On another note. Are you going to church tomorrow? Yes, I know you have a twelve-hour shift on Thursday, but it's a night one. I'll bring you food, or we can get food after.*

> **Me**: *Is this you asking or Kehlani? Because I feel like my darling Kiki put you up to this.*

141

Kayden: Maybe she did. Maybe she didn't. If she did though, is it working?

Me: Surprisingly, yes. But, your bribery tactics did not work. I was planning on going anyway, but I will still take the food.

Kayden: Man, I should've waited to see if you were going first. In the case that you already decided you were going, we're just going to go get food after.

Me: Fine. But I expect a coffee when I get there.

Kayden: You're joking right? Why not just go get one before? It's literally the day before.

Me: Because why would I go get a coffee myself when I have you to do it for me? Fine, I'm joking, I don't need coffee. I do need to go to bed.

Kayden: Alright. See you tonight. Bring your Bible this time.

I'm in bed ready to fall asleep when I get off the phone. *Oh no... I'm smiling at his text messages. That's not good.*

Chapter 19

"Kehlani! What is taking you so long?" I yell when my best friend still hasn't left her room even though she is the one who keeps hounding me to leave that instant.

I can hear her running around, and when she finally steps out of her room, confusion fills my face. "Why are you in full makeup and too-nice-for-a-casual-Wednesday outfit? Usually, you're just in casual jeans or sweats."

"Because I'm going out with Theo after instead of with everyone else. So if you want to take your car you can, or…" She trails off.

I groan in response, "You know as well as I do that my car's got a flat. By the way, you're still driving me to work tomorrow." Kehlani gives me a hopeful look, so I give in, "Fine. I'll ask Kayden or Ashton to drive me home."

Excited, Kehlani gives me a hug, squealing, "Thank you! Thank you! Thank you!" We then bolt out the door to get to church.

When we get to church, we look around for our friends before sitting down. Kehlani sits between Theo and me. As I'm sitting down, Kayden hands me a cup and a pastry bag, "Here, we can't have you hungry and falling asleep during service.

The shock must be evident on my face, "Did you

actually buy me a coffee and some food?" I start laughing, "I was joking, you didn't need to get me any of this."

Kayden just smiles innocently, "I had no idea you were joking." The look on his face tells me otherwise, "I thought you actually wanted it."

"Thank you," I say, and before he can respond, the lights turn down, and worship starts.

For the next hour and a half, we sit and listen to Pastor Jason preach in Romans 12:2 about how we are to be a light in the world. We are to act like and imitate Jesus. What Kayden had commented on my argument with Damien on Monday makes sense now.

After the service, Kehlani and Theo quickly leave, heading to who knows where. As Ashton, Kayden, and I are about to leave, we are stopped by a female voice. "Hello, my dears!"

"Hi, Mom." Kayden says as Ashton and I say, "Hi, Mrs. Kaiser."

Kayden and Theo's mother jogs to catch up to us, pausing when she sees me. "Oh hello, darling. I didn't know you were going to be at church today."

I smile lightly, "Yeah, Kayd, Theo, Kehlani, and Ashton have convinced me to come to church quite a few times in the last month."

Catching me off guard, Mrs. Kaiser pulls me into a hug. "I'm elated that you decided to start coming to church. I do hope that you will continue to attend. That offer to join my Bible study with Kehlani still stands."

As though he can tell his mother is about to start rambling, Kayden cuts in, "Okay Mom, she just started coming here. Let her adjust to it first, then you can bombard her with your questions and hugs." He's gently prying his mother off of me.

Brooklyn takes that moment to walk over to us, "Mom, are you hugging someone for an uncomfortably long

144

time again? You can't do that to people. It makes things awkward."

"I'm a woman of a certain age, Brooke. It's no longer awkward. Maybe if I had grandchildren, I could have my fair share of hugs." Both Kayden and Brooklyn blush.

Brooklyn counters, "Yes, well, that's up to Kayden. I'm nineteen. I have no plans for that in the near future."

Everyone turns to Kayden, who is still blushing. "Nope, not anytime soon." *Is it weird that my heart kind of sinks when I hear that?*

Mrs. Kaiser then starts fussing over Ashton, with Kayden laughing in the background. Brooklyn and I start talking to each other, stepping away from the others.

"So how are you adjusting to college?"

"I'm good actually. It's been an amazing sophomore year. The second semester's back in full swing, and the people are awesome. Wish I could say the same about the administration though."

The last sentence piques my interest, "What's wrong with the administration?"

Brooke sighs before answering, "They've been bringing in speakers that we don't share the same beliefs with. For example, they've brought in some liberal speakers, and for several classes, it was mandatory attendance."

This surprises me, "Huh, I guess I never realized it had gotten that bad. You go to a Christian college though, right?"

She nods, " Yeah, I go to CLU. And it has definitely gotten quite a bit worse. I think at some point in a couple weeks they're bringing in an anti-law enforcement organization." We both snort and then Brooke continues, "My friends and I are definitely protesting that one. Mom and Dad would be pissed if I didn't."

"Does this group have a history of being violent or are they just vocal about their dislike of the police?" I

145

question.

"I believe they go under the name of the COE, but I don't know anything about their history of violence. You might want to make sure there's an officer on duty somewhere near there that day though." She explains.

I haven't heard of that group before. "So this is a newer group?"

Brooklyn nods, "I believe so. I actually think that they're doing a presentation at CLU in hopes of convincing some new college graduates to join their cause. I also believe that they just recently created this branch in this city."

"Oh, that makes sense. Would you mind letting either your father or me know when the class is?" I ask.

She nods and agrees with me before we rejoin the other two, Kayden having left. The five of us talk for a couple more minutes before we decide that we're hungry, and want to go eat.

"So where'd Kayden go? And is he coming with us to get dinner? Are we going to get dinner?"

Ashton chuckles, "Slow your roll. One question at a time. Kayden went to talk to Sage, so you're driving with me. If you want to get dinner, then yes we will go, and Kayden will join us there. If not then, I'll drop you off at home."

I just shrug, "Alright, sounds good. Now let's go get some food. I'm cold."

When they get into the car and start driving, there's a comfortable bit of silence until Ashton speaks up, "Are you and Kayden something?"

I shake my head. *Am I disappointed?* "No? We're not anything. I mean he and I have talked a lot more lately. He's been walking me through this whole Jesus thing.. It's not anything though."

"I think he likes you, you know."

My head whips towards Ashton, "No, no I did not in fact know."

146

Ashton chuckles, "I thought it was so obvious. I thought it was obvious to everyone that you two would end up together. Kiki and I made a bet on when it would happen. I think Mr. and Mrs. Kaiser along with Brooklyn placed a bet on you two as well."

I roll my eyes, "Do you people have nothing better to do than bet on something nonexistent?"

Ashton smirks, "Well, we already know that something's up with Theo and Kehlani. Neither me nor Brooklyn have anything going on with our lives, so why not? But back to my point, you've caught Kayden's eye since the first day you two met. The only reason he hasn't asked you out yet was because you hadn't accepted Christ."

Excuse me? "Are you joking? So he wanted me to be Christian just so he could ask me out?" I can't believe it.

Ashton rolls his eyes with incredulity, "No? Are you thinking straight? Does that seem like something he would do?" I sigh and shake my head, so he continues, "I'm saying that he's probably liked you for a while, but being Christian means that the partner you chose should be equally yoked to you. Plus, I don't think you nor he have even realized you like each other."

I didn't respond. The long pause went on for a bit, until Ashton breaks the silence, "Do you like him, Adria? Be honest with me."

I don't hesitate, "Maybe? I mean, I've never met anyone like him. You can ask Kehlani. I'm always in pure disbelief at anything he does for me. I haven't considered anything with him, and I'm sure he hasn't either."

Ashton takes a deep breath, "I'll give you some advice. First off, pray about it because that in itself is the most important part of a relationship. It must first be built on God. Secondly, make sure this is something you want because it would break Kayden if you led him on."

Silently, I nod, agreeing to follow the advice that

147

Ashton just gave me, "I don't think that we're at that point in our relationship yet. I don't think either of us knows what we want, so I'll just continue hanging out with him and doing the Bible studies. Plus, this is all an assumption, so nothing's happening."

"Makes sense, but you better thank me at you guys' wedding."

Smiling, I say, "Your advice is good, and you're sweet." I decide to tease him, "Why don't you have a girlfriend yet? I know most girls would love to have someone as mature and kind as you as their boyfriend."

Ashton smiles lightly before answering, "Because it isn't God's timing yet. I'm just waiting on him to send me the girl, or make sure I'm in the right place to pursue something with her."

Our little safe bubble bursts when we arrive at the restaurant.

God, please give me the wisdom to know what to do with Kayden. I don't know what to do. If he's the man I am supposed to be with, would you just make sure that we both keep our eyes focused on you? Help me to walk through this with your guidance.

"Hi, sweetheart," Kayden says when he sneaks up on me at the church. We had gotten there early to talk about our weekly study.

I jump up from my seat and hug him. The conversation I had with Ashton is still stuck in the back of my mind. I push it away though.

The two of us start discussing Romans 10:9-10.

148

"When it says you have to accept Jesus, does that mean verbally, or just mentally?" I ask.

"Have you done it mentally?" Kayden returns.

I think for a moment, "No, I mean, I didn't really know. I didn't know I had to accept Jesus. I do believe that He died on the cross for us."

"It seems like you have accepted Him, but if you want we can do a prayer. The prayer isn't magical or anything. It's just a normal prayer, but it's a symbol of your dedication to Christ." He proposes.

I nod my head, wanting to dedicate my life to God. Kayden smiles, "This is the moment I've been waiting for since we've met. Now, repeat after me.

"Dear Heavenly Father, I want to commit my life to you," I repeat after Kayden.

"I know I'm a sinner and have fallen short of Your requirements."

"God, I want to accept You into my heart."

"I believe in my heart that You sent Your son."

"That He died on the cross for my sins."

"Rose again three days later, to save me."

"I place my life into Your hands."

"And in Jesus' name, I pray, Amen."

Once I repeat the 'Amen', Kayden quickly lunges forward to give me a hug, holding me tight. *Is it weird that I don't mind this?* We stay in this position for a couple of minutes, and once we let go, I sigh a breath of relief. "Thank you, Kayd," I whisper.

"No problem, sweetheart." *Well, this is new. Also, why does him calling me sweetheart no longer make me upset?* "You don't know how excited I am for you, or just how excited all the others will be when you tell them. We've all been praying for you, for years. I'm just glad that you've softened your heart towards God."

I give him another hug, "Well thank you for not

149

giving up on me. I know I wasn't the ideal person to listen to your talks about Christianity."

"Oh that is extremely true," He teases. "I'm kidding. But I will say one thing, hold on to your faith, even through the difficulties. God is going to use you for great things."

Kayden's still holding me, and I close my eyes and whisper, "I actually really hope so."

Chapter 20

"Happy Birthday!" Kehlani yells as she bounds into my room, waking me up.

I groan into my pillow, "It's Tuesday, and I don't have to get up for another hour and a half. Let me sleep."

"It's your birthday, get up. I need to leave for work soon, so get up so I can give you your gift." The girl practically jumps onto my bed.

I try shoving her off the bed, "Exactly! It's my birthday! I want to sleep. It's Tuesday, the middle of the week, and I worked last weekend. Let me sleep. We can celebrate on Friday when I have the day off. Or after work."

"Get up, come on. Up."

I groan and get up, "Fine. If I'm grumpy for the rest of the day, this is on you. Did you at least make coffee?"

"Yep, now let's go." The two of us head to the kitchen.

When I walk in, the colorful bouquet catches my eye. I pick up the card on the counter, to see who sent them.

"Awww, thank you, Kiki. Say thank you to Theo for me too. These are beautiful." The different flowers' aroma fills the room.

Kehlani jumps to give me a hug, "Happy Birthday, my best friend, I hope this March second is the best one you've ever had." She smiles and hands me a wrapped

151

present along with a coffee.

"Can every day be my birthday? I don't mind being given flowers and coffee every morning." We both chuckle, "Thank you for the gift."

She starts jumping up and down, "So open it!"

I start laughing, "You're more excited than I am." I start ripping open the paper, and then the box. Inside there's a beige hoodie with the words, 'Powered By Ice Coffee' written in bubble letters on the back. There's also a graphic design tee. "Thank you! These are amazing." I'm still laughing at the hoodie. "This is one of my favorite gifts I have ever been given. I will wear the hoodie all the freaking time."

Kehlani smiles, and says, "Well that phrase is true. You couldn't live without coffee, but there's one more thing inside the box."

I check the box one more time, and this time I notice a pair of jeans at the bottom. When I take the jeans out, I burst into laughter. "You didn't."

Kehlani nods while laughing, "Yes, I did get you those hideous baggy jeans with blue and frayed stars."

"Don't say that. The jeans are the cutest things I've ever seen in my entire life. But thank you for going against your will to get me something I really wanted even if you hate them." I say and hug her back. We spend the rest of the morning eating, and talking to each other.

The Teenage Brained Adults

Theo: Happy Birthday Ria!
Ashton: Happy Birthday, Adria!
Kehlani: Yeah! Happy Birthday.
Again.

Kayden: *Happy Birthday!*
> **Me**: *Thanks y'all! And thank you for the flowers, Theo! And Kiki, but I already said thanks.*

Theo: *I got you flowers?*

Kehlani: *Yes, you did. We placed the order for her when we went out last Wednesday.*

Ashton: *How do you forget going to a flower shop and placing an order? Nonetheless writing the message on the card.*

Kayden: *Are you really surprised that he forgot? Or that he didn't write anything on the card and it was all Kehlani?*

Ashton: *Valid.*

Theo: *Hey!*

> **Me**: *Why am I not surprised? Thanks for pretending like you bought me flowers, and took credit for Kehlani's efforts.*

Kehlani: *The fact that Theo didn't even know he paid for flowers aside, what are we doing for your birthday?*

> **Me**: *Nothing?*

Ashton: *You're funny. We're doing something even if it's just going out for dinner after church or something.*

Theo: *Can you tell we just want a reason to go out?*

Kehlani: *Theo! You can't say the quiet part out loud.*

153

Me: As if I didn't know any of that. You guys can make plans. Just tell me the dates and the time, and I can probably be there.
Kehlani: *Alright. We'll figure it out. See you!*

Later when I get to work, there's another bouquet sitting on my desk. *Lotus flowers. And they're in the prettiest arrangement I've ever seen.* I check the desk, and there's a note there.

Happy Birthday, sweetheart. I'm so glad that you've joined our friend group. Hope you have a good birthday! I'll give you your gift when you have 'your' party. - Kayd

Is it weird that I absolutely melt when I read the message? No? Good, because I do, and it's a very sweet message. *Oh my gosh, I do like him...*

During my lunch break, I decide to call Kayden.

"Hey birthday girl, what's up." He says when he answers the call.

"Hi, I just wanted to say thank you for the flowers. They're beautiful. You didn't need to get me anything."

I can almost hear Kayd smiling over the phone, "I didn't need to buy them, but I saw them and they reminded me of you. Plus, every girl deserves flowers on her birthday."

Dear Lord, I'm blushing over the phone. "I don't know what else to say to that. Thank you. I love them."

"I'm glad you do. Did the others decide on a date to go out for your birthday?" He asks. "I had to go back to work, so I didn't get to see."

"Yeah, they did. I guess we're going out on Friday since I have work off that day. Can you make that day?"

"Hm, let me check my work schedule. I think that

154

day works out. I've been working for the last six, seven days, so we should be good."

"Awesome. I'll make Kehlani figure everything out. I don't have the energy to deal with any of this, and Kiki enjoys that type of thing." I say before we continue talking.

"Are you and Damien good now?" He asks.

I sigh at the mention of my estranged friend, "Yeah, I apologized, and he said we're good, but we haven't spoken to each other since that day. It's different, and it kind of sucks, but in a way, I'm glad that I discovered the way he acts when someone doesn't agree with him."

"Maybe that's God removing him from your life because he's fulfilled his purpose in your life. I'm sure he made a big impact in your life, but if he were to stop helping you grow, I think God removed him for a reason."

Actually, what Kayden says makes me think, and he's right. "Yeah, that's true. I think that even though it hurts, it's for a good reason."

I check the clock, and I realize that my lunch break is almost over. "Wait hold on, aren't you at work? How are you on the phone with me."

Kayden chuckles, "When I saw your call, I knew we were going to talk for a bit, so I decided to take my break, that is almost over. I've got to go. I'll see you tomorrow before church?"

I smile, even though I know he can't see me, "Sounds good, I need to get back too. I'll see you tomorrow."

Oh, I am screwed.

<hr/>

Ashton: Hey, are you going with Kehlani to the diner tomorrow?

Me: No, I think I'll drive there by myself. Kehlani has to work late

tomorrow.
Ashton: *Want to go with me? I think I have to pass by your house on the way.*

Me: *Yeah, sure. Thank you. I'll see you tomorrow.*

Knock. Knock. Knock. "Hold on Ashton! I'll be there in a second." I quickly throw on my cropped white tee, and a pair of baggy jeans.

I open the door, holding my shoes, and my mouth drops open. *Kayden?* "Hey? What are you doing here? I thought Ashton was taking me to the restaurant tonight."

Kayden smiles, "Hey sweetheart, mind if I come in?"

"Yeah, of course, come in. What's happening? Why are you here? I thought you were working. Why are you holding more flowers? Oh, thank you for the lotus flowers. They're gorgeous. I left them at work because they looked good on my desk." I start rambling.

I can tell that Kayden's trying not to laugh. "I'll answer all your questions. I'm here to surprise you. You're welcome for the lotus bouquet. I didn't even notice they weren't here. I thought you would've left them at work since that's where I had them delivered. And I brought more flowers for you," I just then notice that he's now holding a bouquet of pink rose arrangements.

When I take the flowers, I smile a little, they're absolutely gorgeous, "Thank you, I love them. Hold up, I'm going to go put them in a vase."

"Sounds good, just let me know when you're ready to go. We're not in any rush, I got here early." Kayden says as I'm walking towards the kitchen.

When I get back, I realize Kayden never answered

my question, "How come you're here, and not Ashton, not that I'm not happy you're here… and I'm rambling again." Kayden's full-on laughing at this point.

"Well, Ashton asking if he could take you was really just a cover-up for me. I came over because I wanted to ask you if you wanted to go out on a date next weekend." He asks with full confidence.

I'm in shock because, huh? "I… uh… what"

"You don't have to give me an answer now, but I wanted to ask you out, at least not in front of the others."

"I'm so sorry. I didn't mean it like that. I would love to go out with you. I was just caught off guard. I didn't think you were going to ask me out." *AHHHH! Can you tell I'm panicking, and freaking out just a little?*

Kayden smiles and pulls me into a hug. *God, he smells good.* "Awesome. I'll pick you up next Saturday, and we can go now once you put on your shoes." Once I do, we both get into the car and start driving to the restaurant.

As soon as I get out of the car, I instantly regret not bringing a jacket. I start shivering when I meet Kayden to walk in.

"Cold?" He asks when he notices the goosebumps on my skin.

I nod, "Yeah, I regret not bringing a jacket."

"Here, take mine, I'll be fine." He then puts his jacket on my shoulders. I instantly warm up, and I'm not sure if it's because of the jacket, or if it's because of the sweet gesture.

"You sure?"

He nods, "Yeah, if I get cold, then I'll just hug you."

"Really? That was cheesy as heck." *But it made me smile.*

He smirks, "But it works, and it's true, so you'll be fine."

I roll my eyes, "Okay, sure. Now, we've been standing here for about five minutes, and it's only getting colder, so

157

let's go meet our friends."

Smiling, Kayden pulls me into his arms. *Is there anything he does that's not perfect?* "Great, now let's go meet our friends."

I smile and say, "And watch all of them freak out and collect their winning bets on when you or I would ask the other out."

"Yep, that's going to be fun. Hold it! They placed bets on us?" He asks.

I snort, "Are you surprised? Your parents are in on it too. So are our sisters for that matter."

He groans as we walk through the door. *This is awesome.*

Chapter 21

"Ria! Up! Get out of bed. You need to get ready for your date. I have the perfect outfit for you." Kehlani then throws a black-long sleeved shirt, and a cream t-shirt with mushrooms on it, which I assume goes over the black one onto my bed.

My best friend is now rummaging through my closet, to find pants, throwing the clothes she disapproves of onto the floor. After a couple of seconds, she finds a pair of black mom jeans, and a belt, before tossing them at me. "Now go change."

I'm still lying on my bed, and I'm about to burst into laughter. As I'm getting up, I say "Why are you more excited for me to go on a date with Kayd than I am? And why do you care so much about my outfit? It's just Kayden. He's never really cared what I wear."

"Well duh. He's too nice for that. Of course, he wouldn't judge you. But have you met him? He always dresses nicely, and I know you well enough that if you wore whatever you were planning to wear, you would've come home complaining that you weren't dressed up enough."

She's not wrong, so I give in and put on the outfit. When I get out, Kehlani decides that she wants to do my hair. My makeup though is where I draw the line, I will be

159

doing that myself.

As she's trying to put my hair up in a half up half down style, my best friend starts complaining, "Your wavy hair is impossible to style sometimes. If it's not damp, then it starts frizzing up."

I roll my eyes, "How do you think I feel? I have to do my hair every day." Kehlani fake gasps dramatically. "Now, be grateful for your pin-straight, bleach blonde, but still somehow healthy hair."

"At least you tan well, and don't burn if you're in the sun for a couple of hours." she throws back. *True, and I am eternally grateful for that.*

Ding. Dong. The doorbell rings as I'm still doing my makeup. "Hurry up. Hurry up. Hurry up. I want to see you two together." Kehlani urges me.

"Leave me alone. Why are you more excited than I am? Calm down." *Ding. Dong.* "I'm now leaving you and your very hyper self to go get the door.

When I open the door, Kayden's standing there smiling, holding another bouquet out for me. This time they're poppies. "Hey, sweetheart. Are you ready to go?" He greets.

I just look at him for a second, examining the slacks and loose, white button-up he's wearing with the top buttons undone. Smiling, I say, "Yeah, come on in. I need to grab my purse."

He hands me the flowers after hugging me, and I swear, my heart melts right then and there. "Thank you for the flowers. They're gorgeous. Our house is going to turn into a greenhouse if you keep bringing me more."

"Does that mean you want me to send you some every day?" He teases. His face becoming serious, Kayden shrugs, "They're pretty, and they make you smile, so I'll keep bringing them."

"Ahhh! You guys are so cute!" Kehlani squeals from

160

the side of the room, scaring me. Her phone is up, and I just know she's taking pictures.

I roll my eyes as I walk over to put the flowers beside the ones Kayden brought me last week. "How long have you been standing there watching us and taking pictures?"

"Long enough that I have enough blackmail material for both of your sisters to last them a lifetime," Kehlani responds, smirking.

I groan, and Kayden just shrugs, "I'm pretty sure Brooklyn had something to do with at least part of this, so…"

"Can we go now? Before she gets more pictures?" I ask. Kayden nods in agreement before grabbing my hand. We run out the door before she tries to run out and embarrass us.

"Bye Kiki! If I found out you sent any of those pictures to Ashton and Theo, you will be dead! Love you!" I yell as I run out.

Once we get in the car I speak up, "Hey, just so you know. I'm actually on call right now. I don't think I would get called in unless they need quite a few officers on the scene. I just thought you'd want to know. I get it if you want to reschedule."

Kayden rolls his eyes, "That sounds fine. We're still going, and I'll take you home if you get called in."

I nod, "Thank you. Sooo… I know you wouldn't tell me where we're going for the last week… Any chance that will change right now?" I try.

He just smirks, "Nice try, but no. I'm not telling you anything except that putting your hair up is a good thing."

We talk throughout the rest of the drive. When we get there, there's an empty field with a couple of trees surrounding the car. "Did you ask me out on a date just so you could kill me and leave my body in the woods?"

We both start laughing, "No sweetheart. Check the trunk, you'll see."

161

"Stop calling me sweetheart."

"I already asked you on a date, I can call you sweetheart. Now open the trunk already."

I'm confused, but I do as he says. There's a basket in there. "What are we doing?"

"Open the basket."

Looking inside the basket, I start smiling, "We're going on a picnic?"

"Yes, ma'am" he confirms.

I'm surprised, and I know I show it on my face, "Where did you get the idea to do this?"

Kayden looks a little sheepish, "I might have asked Brooklyn to look for ideas on things you'd like to do on our date.

That's the cutest thing I've ever heard. "You are absolutely ridiculous in the best way possible." He smiles shyly, and grabs my hand, and the basket before pulling me to find a spot to set up.

When we find a place in a field filled with flowers, he sets up the checkered blanket and takes out the food.

Before we start to eat, Kayden offers to pray. "Dear heavenly father, I pray that You would bless this food we are about to eat, and let it nourish our bodies. God, I pray that You would bless this date that we're on, and guide us through this new territory. And finally, I pray that You would allow us to go on more dates in the future." I start giggling when I hear the last sentence. "And in Jesus' name, I pray, Amen."

"Great, now can we eat? I'm hungry, and Kehlani decided to torture me into getting ready for two hours instead of letting me eat breakfast." I say trying to break the ice.

Kayden laughs, "She, Theo, Ashton, and our families do seem to be more excited that we're on this date than we are. But if it helps you look beautiful, so whatever she did paid off."

162

I feign annoyance, "Are you saying I don't normally look good?"

Kayden rolls his eyes, "That's not what I'm saying. I'm saying…"

I cut him off, "I know what you're saying. I'm just teasing you. You look good too."

Kayden grins and pulls me into a hug. He then kisses me on the forehead. *Please help me. I'm actually melting right now.* "Thank you. Now come on, let's eat."

For the next couple of hours, we sit there talking about our friends, family, and God. The time passes by quickly, and it's honestly the best date I've ever been on. *I want this to happen again.*

I sigh, "I wish my mom were here to hear about this, and to meet you."

Kayden pulls me into a hug, "I know you do. She would be happy for you."

"I know she would. She would've loved to meet you. She'd been hounding me on getting a boyfriend, or to start dating." I giggle.

"Boyfriend?" Kayd asks, his eyebrows raised.

I roll my eyes then ask as we lie on the blanket, sunbathing, "So…what are we then, Kayd?"

Kayden sighs as he pushes himself up on his elbows before turning to look at me, "Well, what if we're dating, and I'm your boyfriend."

I smirk before pushing myself to sit up straight, "Well, that sounds like something I'd be into, but you haven't asked yet, so…"

He rolls his eyes playfully, "Really? I have to ask formally? Alright then," Kayd then gets up and onto one knee like a proposal. "Adria Juliette Sousa, will you do me the honor of being my girlfriend." We're both giggling. "Does this work for you?"

I'm nearly dying from laughter, "You're such a

163

dork, but yes that works, and yes I would love to be your girlfriend."

Kayden goes back to sitting, and I hug him, and he kisses my head. We sit there for a while, until my phone rings.

I sit up to grab my phone and check my messages.

Brooklyn: Hey Ria. I'm so sorry. I completely forgot to get back to you. The COE speaker is coming out to CLU at 4 p.m. It's going to be outside by the auditorium. It sounds like a decent amount of students I know are going. I don't know if it's to protest or attend, but I found out they've had a history of violence in the past. Sorry again for getting back to you so late.

Me: Thank you so much. I will tell your father, and maybe see you there.

"Hey, Kayd, hold on, I need to call your Dad for something regarding work. Give me a second." When he nods, I get up to call Chief Kaiser.

On the second ring, he picks up, "Hello Officer Sousa. Is there an issue?"

"Hey Chief, Brooklyn just texted me to inform me that there's a COE speaker who's giving a presentation at her university. Apparently, they have a history of violence. They're trying to establish a branch in this part of California. Are there any officers that you can place on patrol in that area?" I say.

There's some shuffling over the phone before he

164

responds, "Let me check. I don't think I have more than one of two that could head over there right now. You're on call, aren't you? I know you're on a date with Kayden right now, but is there any way you could head down there?"

I sigh. I don't really want to leave, but the reminder of the oath I swore when I became an officer makes me push that thought away. "Yeah, I can come in. The speech doesn't start for another hour or two. I should be back to the station in about an hour to an hour and a half."

"Okay, yeah. I will need you to come in. I have one officer that I could send, but he would only be a backup should you need it." Chief Kaiser reports, "I will see you in a bit then. Thank you for the information."

When he hangs up, I look at Kayden disappointed, and I know he already knows, "So, I'm guessing you heard everything.

Kayden nods and starts to get up, pack up the blankets, and the leftover food. "Yep. Come on, I'll take you home."

"I'm so sorry. I didn't know that the speech was today. I promise. I'll make it up to you. We can go out again tomorrow after church or something. I'm so so sor—" My rambling is cut off when Kayden gives me a quick kiss.

I freeze as he smirks at me, "Great, now that you've stopped talking. I can tell you that I don't mind taking you home. You have a job, and you have to do it. We can always go out another day. So let's go."

Still speechless, I simply nod.

I still haven't said anything even after Kayden puts the basket back in the trunk and gets into the driver's seat. Kayd starts laughing at me, "Oh my goodness. You're still speechless. If I knew that was the way to get you to stop rambling, I would've kissed you sooner."

I crack a smile, and then hit him as I snap out of my thoughts, "Shut up, and start driving." He does as I say.

When we get back to my house, Kayden walks

165

me inside, and while I get ready, he sits on the couch with Kehlani.

Once I've changed, I give him a hug, and say to him and Kehlan, "Okay, now I really have to go. I will see you later, I hope. Anyways, both of you, pray that nothing gets too violent.

"We will." They agree as I hug Kehlani, and give Kayden a quick kiss.

Kehlani's jaw drops, so I roll my eyes and say, "Yes, you saw me kiss him. We can talk about it when I get back. Now bye." With that, I run out the door, and head to the station.

Chapter 22

"*What* time is the speaker going to get on stage?" I ask Brooklyn over the phone while I'm sitting inside the patrol car near the outdoor auditorium.

There is a murmur through the phone before Brooklyn says, "In like fifteen minutes. I think he's going to be late. The presentation shouldn't be longer than an hour, to be honest, so if you're here to observe, or make sure nothing happens, I'd say show up in like forty-five minutes."

When I do get out of the car, I start walking towards the loud talking in the stands. *I hope that nothing happens.* As I get closer, I can hear the presenter yelling passionately into the mic. "Law enforcement should be here to protect us, but what have they done for us recently? The Christian Galloway Shooting is a perfect example of that. They killed him rather than shooting him in a nonfatal area. Had the officers had better aim, he would have been stopped earlier. They killed him rather than shooting him non-fatally. Not just that, but they could have taken the opportunity to push a gun ban."

The crowd starts to murmur as he continues, "What did they do instead? They advocated for the keeping of guns legal in California. How is that an example of protection or Justice?"

Why does that voice sound so familiar? Who is that speaking?
As I walk closer, the stage and people come more clearly into sight. *Oh. My. Gosh. That's... No. Why would he? Damien? What the heck?*
My heart breaks for a moment. I had no idea he felt that strongly against law enforcement. I pull out my phone to text Kehlani. I just need to tell someone.

> *Me: Kiki... The speaker at CLU is Damien. He's part of the COE. I've been trying to figure out who's the head of the Silver Valley Branch, and it's him. I can't believe that he would do something like this.*

God, please just help me right now to be able to keep my composure. Please just help guide me through this. I don't know what to do. And please help keep everyone safe here.
I then start walking through the campus trying not to cause or draw attention. When I finish circling the area I decide to walk back to the auditorium. Brooklyn and her friends catch my eye when I see them standing nearby, silently protesting the event.
"Thank you all for your time and your hospitality. It was great speaking here, and I hope that you guys will do more research into the topics I have mentioned. If you would like to join or donate to the COE, come meet me at the table." Damien says as he finishes his speech. I just watch with disappointment.
Brooklyn spots me once he finishes the presentation, and runs over to me giving me a hug. "I'm so sorry that he did that to you. I can't believe that a close friend did that to you."
Once he is finished speaking to the students at his

168

booth, I storm over to him, "How dare you? And how could you? You're part of an organization that wants me to get fired? Are you joking?"

His face turns cold, and his words are like ice, "Hello Officer. I just want what's best for the citizens of this country, and this current form of law enforcement is the opposite of that. That is why the Change Of Enforcement Organization was created. We as people are allowed to have our own opinions.

I knew that he didn't love law enforcement, but knowing that he would go this far as to join an organization that has a history of violence hurt. The final blow for me was that he would pretend that he didn't know me. Taking a deep breath, all I say is, "Thank you for speaking to me sir, I will get out of the way now."

That hurt. But on the bright side, at least the event is over without any physical or violent damage.

BANG! BANG! BANG!

I curse under my breath. *I guess I spoke too soon.* I turn to run behind the stage, and when I peak out, I see bullets starting to fly and screams filling the air.

I pick up my radio and speak into it saying, "There's a 10-71 in progress at CLU. The motive is unknown, but there was an anti-law enforcement event that was just held on campus by an organization that has a previous history of violence.

"MOVE TO FIND A SHELTER!" I yell at the remaining students still in the outside auditorium. "HIDE INSIDE A ROOM, OR ANYTHING, JUST GET OUT OF THE OPEN!"

With that, I start running towards the shots, determined to find the person who is risking the safety of the students here.

BANG! BANG! BANG! BANG!

The person shooting is shooting at my patrol car.

169

"Shooter wearing a beige t-shirt. Holding a gun. Likely a Glock. Currently shooting." *Dang it. That is one of the students Damien was speaking to earlier. What the heck did Damien say to him?*

I take out a Glock 48, and slowly start creeping towards the man, hiding behind some cars. I stop about fifty feet away from him. "PUT THE WEAPON DOWN NOW!" I bellow.

BANG! BANG!

The man clearly doesn't listen, so I hold my gun out towards him while yelling out to the several remaining people in the area. "GET OUT OF THIS AREA NOW!"

The man stops firing before turning around to face me. He's got a deranged look on his face. "Look, it's the person who was supposed to protect all these people."

Out of the corner of my eye, I notice that Brooklyn is trying to move people out of the open, so I speak to the man trying to distract him.

"Sir, please put the gun down, or I will have to shoot. Please put down the gun." He then lifts the gun towards me and holds it there.

The man smiles wickedly, "I will not. You have done enough! Leave!"

"Sir, you've already injured several people, please put the gun down." He does for a second before holding the gun back up towards me. "I will have to shoot if you don't put the gun down."

After seconds that drag on like years, I see movement in my peripheral vision. I continue to plead with the man to put down his gun, knowing that if I shot right now, he would be able to fire just as quickly.

The movement I see is the second officer, and he starts slowly creeping closer towards us. I continue to speak and plead to the man, in the hopes that either he would drop the gun, or not notice the second officer, and give him an opportunity to shoot him.

The fifty feet between the shooter and I seems to shrink as time very slowly moves. All I can do is hope and pray that God will place his protection over me.

God, please would you place your protection over me, and help me through this time. Please give me the strength to stand up, and protect all these people. Help those injured right now, and if it's my time to go home, let me stop the shooter first.

I'm hyper-aware of everything around me. Although I could shoot now, and so could the other officer, we wait for a couple more seconds in the hopes that Brooklyn can get the remaining people out of the open area.

The second officer has moved somewhere close enough to aim his shot, and where his stray bullets wouldn't reach me. I try one more time.

"SIR, I AM GOING TO TELL YOU ONLY ONE MORE TIME, DROP YOUR WEAPON, OR I WILL NOT HESITATE TO SHOOT," I yell. *Please, God, give me strength right now.*

The shooter smirks with a psychotic glint in his eyes. He then loads the gun and aims it at me.

Oh God, save me. Give me strength.

I close my eyes waiting for the shots to fire.

BANG! BANG! BANG!

Oh *no.*

Chapter 23

Kayden

She's gone. She's really gone. My heart hurts. My thoughts are being pulled in two different directions. On one hand, I hate that she was taken from us when she had the brightest life ahead of her, but on the other hand, I know that she has fulfilled the plan that God had for her. He was ready for her to go back home to see him again.

But if I had known that she was going to be taken from us so soon, I would've said I love you one more time. I would have made a bigger effort to see her more often. I would have hugged her once more, but I can't do any of that anymore. *After everything she's gone through, she was still taken from us. What was your plan with this God?* I walk over to the coffin where her body lies. The peace on her face just reminds me that she is finally in a better place, rejoicing in heaven with her Lord and Savior, but that doesn't stop the tears from pooling in my eyes.

Taking a deep breath before I speak to the crowd

sitting in front of me here to pay their respects, "She was taken from us way too soon. And yes, I truly do wish that we all got to keep her for longer, but God clearly had other plans. Many of us, had we lived the life that she lived, would have folded to the pressure and pain, but she didn't. She was strong, and fought through everything that was thrown her way."

I stop, wanting to compose myself before continuing, "My sister had more life in her than anyone could ever imagine. She may have been seven years younger than me, but she was one of my best friends. I hate that we weren't able to watch her graduate from college or get married, but I am eternally grateful that we got to watch her grow from that shy and reserved girl to the sunshine of the room. Brooklyn was never afraid to share her faith with anyone. She would make so many friends just by being her, and the impact she's made in all of their lives. She died leading people to safety"

I have to stop to keep my tears from falling, "Brookie, I know you're watching us from heaven, and I just want to say, I love you so much. I know you're rejoicing in heaven with Jesus. I cannot thank you for being my little sister through everything. I can't wait to see you again in heaven."

My brain blocks out the soft applause as I walk back to the bench seats. When I sit next to Adria she grabs my hand and whispers, "That was awesome, Kayd. You reminded everyone that this is a celebration of life, a reason to be joyful. Brooklyn would be so proud of you. Both she and Sam are watching you from heaven with God elated that you're using her death as a way to still evangelize."

How she knows what to say at the perfect time, I will never understand, but I'm thankful. "Thank you, sweetheart." I kiss the top of her head, "I miss both of them so much, but I know that they're both happier than ever."

Sadness no longer clouds my mind as the next person goes up to speak. During her speech, I am reminded of all the good times I had with my sister, and by the end of her speech, I was smiling.

When she finishes speaking, to my surprise, Elianna stands up and starts walking towards the podium, "Hi everyone. I know most of you probably don't know me, but I'm Ellie. My older sister is dating Kayden. But we aren't here to talk about them, we're here to talk about Brooklyn. Brooke was four years older than me, and often girls that much older would think that they were too cool to hang out with freshmen, but Brooke wasn't. My mother had just passed away, and I was drowning in all my emotions, Brooke took the time to sort out all those feelings. She was there when it was midnight and I just wished I wasn't here but with my parents instead."

Tears start spilling out of Ellie's eyes as she takes a breath, "Brooke always talked about God, and how being a Christian meant that she knew where she was going after death. When I heard that a stray bullet had hit her, everything she had told me in my eyes was proven false, but as she was fighting for her life on her deathbed, she retold me the story of Christ, and her mission here on Earth. I don't know if I believe it, but I hope with all my heart that she was right and she's with God right now."

Ellie's speech is the last one, and after Pastor Jason prays over the service, we all stand up, ready to see all those who came by to say goodbye to Brooklyn. Adria says something about needing to use the restroom, so when she leaves, I start to say thank all those who have shown up.

"Hey, Kayd." a female voice says while I am speaking to one of my mom's friends.

"Well hi, mini Ria. Where's her other mini?" I asked.

Elianna shakes her head at her nickname, "She's over there talking to your mom. How are you doing? I know it's probably rough having to do a second one of these for both your siblings."

"Well, I'm doing about as well as I can. Thank you for asking. How are you?" I return the question to her.

Elianna shrugs as she sits down, but I can see the pain in her eyes, "Confused. Sad. But I'm okay. It doesn't get any easier does it."

I know she wants to talk about it, "No it doesn't, but it's the way you deal with it that's most important. So what's so confusing?"

"Why are you so okay? She's your sister. I'm not accusing you of anything, I'm just wondering. You've already lost your brother too. Everyone that spoke tonight just accepted that she was gone, because you all believe that God was ready to take her. But why are you ready to accept it? Does it now confuse you that he's supposed to be a good God, but he took a girl in her prime away? How real is he? He already took my parents, and then now he's taking the person who got me through their death." she sighs to me as listing all her concerns.

I sit down next to her, "I get your confusion, I do. I had the same questions when Sam died. I'll try to explain everything as best as I can, but I'm going to tell you the summary. It's all because of the hope that God offers *us*. Okay first off, why or how am I okay? Well for one this is a celebration of life. We're all here to celebrate everything that Brooklyn did while she was with us. Yes, the shooter and the rest of that organization cut her life short, and I would be lying if I said it didn't hurt, but God was ready to take her home. I'm in pain, and hurting because she's gone, but she's in heaven singing and dancing. Brooke's got a new body, the same soul, but a new body, in a place where pain, sadness, and hurt just don't exist. Now, Brooklyn told you the impact Sam's death had, right?"

When she nods, I continue, "She was always sad after he died, and hurt, it got to the point where she went mute for a year or two. It wasn't hard since she was homeschooled,

176

but everything for her hurt. Sam was her best friend. The one she ran to when she was hurt, the one that she would tell if someone was being mean to her, and, what I found out later, the one that she told when she was doubting her faith. When Sam died, I think she basically lost all faith that she had in God, and was feeling a lot like you are right now. I don't know every detail of how she got through it because I wasn't the one who mainly helped her, but I do know that this was the verse that she said constantly ran through her mind."

I stop to get my Bible since I don't know the passage word for word. "I found it. 'For we do not have a High Priest who cannot sympathize with our weaknesses, but was in all points tempted as we are, yet without sin. Let us therefore come boldly to the throne of grace that we may obtain mercy, and find grace to help in time of need.' Hebrews 4:15-16. I think for her this verse reminded her that Jesus knew every single emotion that she was going through. In Jesus' case, King Herod beheaded his cousin John. John was beheaded because he had told Herod that it was sinful for him to take his brother's wife. Herod never wanted to kill John, but after promising his neice anything that she asked of him up to half his kingdom, and her request was John's head on a platter, Herod killed him."

Ellie nods, deep in thought, and I continue, "As another instance, well we both know what Damien did to Ria, right? Well, Jesus had a similar situation. Judas, one of his closest friends, sold Him out to the pharisees' who wanted Him dead for thirty pieces of silver. Judas lived and walked around with Jesus for three years, and all it took was thirty pieces of silver for him to betray Jesus. Jesus knew the pain that we all go through when we lose someone dear to us, and He has the power to help us when we are weak."

"I'll have my mom talk to you later. She knows better than I do. Okay?" I tell her as she sits there seemingly sorting through her thoughts.

"Yeah, that sounds nice," Ellie replies before jumping on me to give me a hug. "Thank you, Kayden. I'm glad Adria decided to date you."

I laugh at her last statement, "You're very welcome Ellie. And I'm glad Ria decided to date me too. Now how about we go find her?"

When she nods, both of us look for her. As soon as we find her talking to Kehlani, we look at each other, coming to a mutual understanding to run over to her. I beat Ellie there, but instead of stopping when I get to Adria, I continue, picking her up and spinning her around.

"Kayden! Put me down right now!" Adria demands as I hold her tight.

I laugh before doing as she demands, "What? I can't give you a hug. You have to be nice to me. We're here for Brooklyn."

"She would've encouraged me to hit you, Kayd. So don't even try to play that card." Adria reminds me with a glare. But after a second a smile breaks through, and I know that she isn't actually mad at me.

"Ellie was asking all the right questions about God earlier," I whisper to Ria. "Seems she has very similar questions that her big sister had. It'd do her good if you talked to her about it."

"I'm glad that she is. I want her to find the peace that He's given me. I just don't know how to talk to her about it. I'll figure it out though." She replies as she grabs my hand to lead us to Theo, Ashton, and Kehlani.

As I follow her I respond, "I know you will. You always do, sweetheart."

"Oh gross. We have to hear you be all sweet to Adria now. Adria, you're not going to be that nice to Kayden right?" Ashton complains. I slap him on the side of the head for that.

"I can't promise I won't. I will still argue with him, or hit him. I'm still me after all." My girlfriend answers as

178

Theo and Ashton groan.

I roll my eyes at their stupidity, "Theo, you're just as bad with Kehlani. Don't start taking Ashton's side. And Ashton, I'll give you a pass since you're lonely and single." That sentence earns me a slap to the head.

"At least we leave room for Jesus and are all cuddly when you guys *aren't* around us. You are always being nice, holding her hand, and giving her every pet name imaginable." Theo tries to defend himself.

Adria immediately snaps back, "That's not true. You guys actually cuddle at every single movie night that we have. Kayd and I haven't even dated long enough for that."

That's my girl.

I look around me to see my dad speaking to the family and friends who came here to celebrate the next stage of life that Brooklyn had entered. My mom is still talking to Charlotte, but Elianna has joined them this time. Adria is talking to Kehlani and Theo, laughing and joking with my father and Ashton. Not everything is perfectly fine, in fact, many of our hearts are still shattered and hurting, but we will get through it. Not by our merit, but by the merit of God who would give us the strength to navigate the grief we all are feeling. We've got each other, and we will help each other heal.

I snap back into reality as Kehlani said to me, "Right, Kayden?"

"Oh-uhm. Right." I say, not really knowing what I have agreed to. As Kehlani and Theo bicker over goodness knows what, I whisper to Adria, who is still in my arms, "I will never stop thanking God that our paths crossed when they did. I cannot wait to see what else he has planned for us during the rest of our lives." And as she agrees with me, I give her a small kiss on the head.

Author's Note

Hey to whoever's reading this! I hope you enjoyed reading this book as much as I enjoyed writing, and daydreaming. Anyways, I'm going under the name Kristen Taylor. This crazy, crazy world makes it hard for teenagers to find good, clean Christian books that have a good plotline. So that's where I come in. I'm here to write books that have popular genres and tropes that appeal to y'all teenagers.

The Bible just happens to say in Luke 21 verses 10 and 11, "Nations will rise against nation, and kingdom against kingdom. There will be great earthquakes, famines, and pestilences in various places, and fearful events, and great signs from heaven." But we're also told in 1st Peter 4 verses 10 and 11 that, "Each of you should use whatever gift you have received to serve others, as faithful stewards of God's grace in its various forms. If anyone speaks, they should do so as one who speaks the very words of God. If anyone serves, they should do so with the strength God provides, so that in all things God may be praised through Jesus Christ. To him be the glory and the power forever and ever. Amen." I believe that this is one way that I can use my talents to spread the light in a dark world.

I hope you enjoyed my book though!

Made in the USA
Las Vegas, NV
14 December 2024